D1024765

# Jessica Haggerthwaite:
# Witch Dispatcher

# Jessica Haggerthwaite:
# Witch Dispatcher

## Emma Barnes

### Illustrations by
### Tim Archbold

Walker & Company • New York

First published in the United States of America in 2001 by
Walker Publishing Company, Inc.

Originally published in Great Britain in 2001 by Bloomsbury
Publishing Plc, 38 Soho Square, London, W1D 3HB

Library of Congress Cataloging-in-Publication Data

Barnes, Emma.
Jessica Haggerthwaite, witch dispatcher / Emma Barnes ;
illustrations by Tim Archbold.
p. cm.
Summary: When her mother decides to start a business as a
professional witch, eleven-year-old Jessica sets out to
sabotage the project.
ISBN 0-8027-8794-0
[1. Witchcraft—Fiction. 2. Family life—Fiction.]
I. Archbold, Tim, ill. II. Title.

PZ7.B2617 Je 2001
[Fic]—dc21
2001026570

Printed in the United States of America

2 4 6 8 10 9 7 5 3 1

*For Lily Cohen and Sylvia Barnes,*
*in memory—E. B.*

*For Louise, Rosie, and John—T. A.*

# Chapter One

"Guess what!" demanded Mrs. Haggerthwaite, bursting through the kitchen door. And before anybody had a chance to respond, she added, "I have the most amazing news!"

The reaction was not all it might have been. Nat, who was tickling Liverwort, hardly looked up. Jessica shot her mother a forbidding glance over the top of the large volume that was propped up in front of her (it was, even more forbiddingly, called *Astrophysics Made Simple*). Liverwort just burped.

But Mrs. Haggerthwaite was not easily put off.

"I'll give you three guesses!"

"You've bought another toad?" Nat suggested. And he made soothing noises at Liverwort, the

Haggerthwaite's toad, in case he should feel threatened by this.

"You've actually found a job?" said Jessica. She looked at her mother and then, meaningfully, at the bills that were stuck to the fridge. Several of them had LAST DEMAND FOR PAYMENT written across the top in large, unfriendly letters. Then she sniffed, to show just how unlikely she thought this was.

"That's it!"

Jessica gasped. Nat stopped tickling Liverwort and gazed at his mother. Even Liverwort gave an enquiring croak.

"I don't believe you," said Jessica. "Who would give you a job? Anyway, I thought you didn't want one. You always say you need all your time for your witching." Not that Jessica approved of this. She thought her mother spent altogether too much time on her witchcraft, and not nearly enough time looking for a sensible job. But that was not the point.

"All right." Mrs. Haggerthwaite came clean. "I haven't exactly got a job. But it's just as good. Actually, it's even better!" She paused for effect. "I'm going to be a professional witch! Mellandra Haggerthwaite, Professional Witch! Doesn't that sound good?"

There was a long, long silence.

Nat looked stunned. In fact, he looked as if
somebody had just crept up and whacked him over
the head with Jessica's *Junior Science Encyclopedia*.
As for Jessica, she had to clutch the table to steady
herself. She was thinking, It's finally happened.

Mom really has gone crazy. But out loud she said, "Mom, you can't have got a job as a professional witch. There *are* no professional witches."

"Exactly!" said Mrs. Haggerthwaite. "That's the beauty of it. I'll be the first one! Why, I shouldn't be surprised if we don't end up millionaires!" She glanced at their dazed faces and exclaimed, "Oh, for goodness sake! Let me get a cup of tea and I'll explain."

According to Mrs. Haggerthwaite, it had all started in the library. She was looking at the job section of the local paper at the time and was in a very bad mood—for while she definitely needed a job, it was also true that she didn't really want one. Looking at the advertisements in the *Bellstone Gazette*, she thought crossly how few jobs there were for somebody with experience in witchcraft, and she couldn't see anything that would fit in with her busy schedule of herb gathering and charm making. She also wondered why there were jobs for cooks and manicurists and dental assistants, but absolutely nothing in the magical line at all.

"And that's when it came to me," said Mrs. Haggerthwaite. "Where do you go if you need magical services? A good-luck charm or a love potion? Or if your house is haunted by your great-aunt's ghost? There isn't anywhere to go. Because there just aren't any professional witches out there. Until now. Because that's where I come in!"

"Mom!" Jessica groaned. "You can't be a professional witch! Everyone will think you're crazy! And what about me and Nat? I mean, what will they say at school?"

"They'll be green with envy!"

"No, they won't! They'll kill themselves laughing. Why, we'll be the biggest joke in Bellstone!"

Mrs. Haggerthwaite had not thought of this. In fact, it had never even occurred to her that there might be something unusual in having a mother who was a witch.

"Jessica! You're not . . . you're not suggesting that I embarrass you?"

She actually looked upset. And suddenly Jessica found that she was unable to say what she had been going to say: that *of course* Mrs. Haggerthwaite embarrassed her, she was probably the most embarrassing mother in the *universe*.

"She doesn't mean it like that, Mom," said Nat, although both he and Jessica knew very well that she did.

"No," said Jessica quickly. "But what about me? You know I'm planning to be a world-famous scientist. That's hard enough, especially if you're a girl. But how many world-famous scientists have you heard of with witches for mothers?"

"Lots," said Mrs Haggerthwaite. Before Jessica could ask her to name one, she added quickly, "Anyway, magic and science aren't as different as you think."

"Of course they are!"

"No, they're not. What do you think really turns the light on when you flip the switch?"

"Electricity," chorused Jessica and Nat.

"And what is electricity, may I ask?"

Nat hesitated. But Jessica said confidently, "Electrons, traveling down a wire."

"And what, may I ask, are electrons?"

"They're bits of atoms. And atoms are very small particles that everything is made from."

"Show me one, then," said Mrs. Haggerthwaite.

"What? But I can't. They're invisible!"

"Invisible? Sounds like magic to me," said Mrs. Haggerthwaite triumphantly.

Jessica scowled. "They're not magic, they're science! Anyway, that's not the point. You can't go into business as a witch. Everyone'll just think you're crazy! And I bet Dad says the same."

"I'm sure he'll think it's an excellent idea," said Mrs. Haggerthwaite. "Just like I did when he set up his own gardening business."

"Well, I think it's a rotten idea!" Jessica shouted, "And I bet Dad does, too. What's more, I'm going to get him and find out!" And she leaped up and ran for the door.

Nat caught up with her as she was running out the gate.

"Stop!" he yelled. "Where are you going, anyway?"

Jessica paused for a moment. "Just to Aunt Kate's. Dad said he was doing some jobs for her this afternoon." Aunt Kate was Mr. Haggerthwaite's sister, and when business was slow she often asked him to look after her vegetable patch or the plants in her greenhouse. Business had often been slow lately.

"There's no point in telling Dad," said Nat. "He'll find out when he gets home." He hesitated. "Anyway, they'll only have another fight."

"Well, at least it'll be a fight about something sensible," said Jessica. She added, "For once."

Nat sighed. It was true that their parents often had fights, and they could be about the stupidest things. For example, once they had had a fight about whether eating carrots gave you dandruff. Another time they had a falling out over whether the capital of Japan was Rangoon or Singapore. (Jessica had settled that one: "It's Tokyo, of course!") But lately they had been fighting more often and always about the same subject: Money and Why There Was Not Enough of It. Nat was getting tired of these arguments.

He looked at Jessica, whose brown eyes were glinting in a way he knew too well. He was sure she

would be a world-famous scientist one day: She was stubborn enough to succeed at anything. But for the moment he wished she would not always be in such a rush.

"Can't you just wait and see what happens?" he asked.

But he was talking to empty air.

# Chapter Two

As she ran down the street, Jessica thought for the thousandth time that it was a terrible nuisance having a witch for a mother.

Other people's mothers had sensible hobbies. They made jam or fixed bikes or practiced the piano. They did not go around pretending they could charm warts, or offer potions for ingrown toenails (potions that they made themselves from pond slime and black beetles). Nor did they dress up in long, black capes and go and practice incantations in the back garden, so that all the neighbors came out and stared, and all the neighbors' kids giggled. Nor did they serve up nettle soup on the grounds that it was "good for the blood."

Other people's mothers met their friends for coffee. Mrs. Haggerthwaite met her friends for witches' conventions and the like. They all wore peculiar clothes and owned peculiar pets ("familiars" they called them), most of which tried to eat Liverwort whenever they saw him. The only good thing was that none of the other witches lived in Bellstone.

It would not be so bad if witchcraft ever achieved anything useful. If, for example, it enabled you to turn ordinary metal into gold or conjure chocolate cake out of thin air—or even did the dishes. But Mrs. Haggerthwaite's magic was not of this type. "I'm not interested in that rough, crude magic," she would declare superiorly. "That is not what real witchcraft is about. Real witchcraft works with Nature to redirect the Cosmic Forces." She was never very precise about what the Cosmic Forces were, however, and secretly Jessica had long ago decided that witchcraft did nothing worthwhile at all.

But at least Mrs. Haggerthwaite's witchcraft had, until now, been carried out in an amateur capacity. Jessica was sure that a professional witch would be much more difficult to hide.

As she ran up the steps to Aunt Kate's, Jessica suddenly wondered whether her father would see things the same way. For the fact was that although

Mr. Haggerthwaite was the most down-to-earth man imaginable, it was almost impossible to get him to come out against Mrs. Haggerthwaite and her witchcraft. He was fond of her, after all, and over the many years of their marriage, he had grown used to defending her. "Now, then," he would say, if Aunt Kate happened to mention "that tomfoolery Mellandra goes in for" or if Jessica complained about pond slime in the fridge. "We're not talking about pointy hats and flying around on a broomstick. No black cats and campfires. We're just talking about a slightly different approach to life. An interest in herbalism. Getting in touch with the spiritual side. An awareness of the mysteries of life."

Perhaps he would not take Jessica's side after all.

Jessica was so worried at this thought that she did not stop to speak to her aunt, even though she was very fond of her, and even though there was a wonderful smell of fresh-baked scones wafting out the window (Aunt Kate was well known as the best baker in Bellstone). Instead she raced around to the back garden and into the greenhouse.

"Dad!" she yelled. "Dad, you'll never guess what's happened!"

Mr. Haggerthwaite was potting some tomatoes. He looked up when he heard Jessica and grinned

his lopsided grin. "Hello, love," he said. "Now what's got you so excited?"

Despite the grin, it seemed to Jessica that he had a worried look around his eyes. He had looked that way a lot recently, ever since he lost his job when the big market garden closed down and he had decided to go into business as a gardener by himself.

"It's Mom," said Jessica. "She's decided to set

up a business. She's going to be a professional witch."

Mr. Haggerthwaite's jaw dropped. "No!"

Jessica nodded. In a rush she told him everything Mrs. Haggerthwaite had said. Mr. Haggerthwaite continued to press in the soil around his tomato plants, but he gave a long, low whistle.

"You've got to hand it to her," he told Jessica. "After fifteen years she still amazes me!"

"So you don't think it's a good idea?" asked Jessica eagerly.

"It's a terrible idea," said Mr. Haggerthwaite cheerfully. "Not only that—it could land us in all sorts of trouble."

"Mom says we'll end up millionaires."

"End up behind bars more like, for defrauding the public. Or she will, anyway, if we don't do something to stop her." Mr. Haggerthwaite rubbed his head thoughtfully, not noticing that he was getting soil all over it. "I don't know. I'm beginning to think this witch business has gone too far. Yesterday she was telling me I should use witchcraft on my tomatoes! I ask you! I've been growing tomatoes for years!"

Jessica nodded solemnly. If Aunt Kate baked the best cakes in Bellstone, then everyone knew Mr. Haggerthwaite grew the best tomatoes.

"She just hasn't thought it through," he said. "That's what it is. But you leave it to me. She'll soon come to her senses."

He put an arm around Jessica, and together they left the greenhouse. Jessica felt happy now that everything was going to be sorted out. But if Nat had been there, he would have told her otherwise. He would have pointed out that Mr. Haggerthwaite was as famous for his tactlessness as Jessica was for always rushing into things—or as Mrs. Haggerthwaite was for never, ever being sensible. And that they all had hot tempers.

He would have told her to expect the worst.

They arrived home to find Mrs. Haggerthwaite sitting at the kitchen table writing a list. She was, in fact, writing a list of all the things she needed to do to become a professional witch, although luckily they did not know this. Nat was sitting next to her, trying to make Liverwort jump over a spoon. But Liverwort was having none of it. He knew that jumping was for frogs, not toads, and was looking at the spoon in a very haughty manner.

When Mrs. Haggerthwaite heard them come in, she looked at them in much the same way that Liverwort was looking at the spoon.

"So has Jessica told you about my wonderful idea?" she asked.

"She's told me you have some harebrained scheme to go into business as a witch," said Mr. Haggerthwaite, seconds before it occurred to him that this was not the most tactful way to begin.

Mrs. Haggerthwaite bristled. "And what's wrong with that, Tom Haggerthwaite?" she snapped. "After all, somebody needs to make some money in this house!" (Tact was not really Mrs. Haggerthwaite's strong point either.)

Mr. Haggerthwaite reddened. He and Nat both had sandy colored hair and very fair, freckled skin, and they both blushed easily. "That's not fair, Melly. I'm doing the best I can. Things will get better. In fact, only today I heard that Bert Flotsam—you know, the one who owns those big hotels—well, he's thinking of having their properties landscaped. Think what a big job that would be! Why, if I got that, then all our troubles would be over!" And for a moment Mr. Haggerthwaite no longer looked cross or worried, but as if his tomatoes had just taken first place in the Bellstone Horticultural Show.

"That may be. Meanwhile, we have bills to pay. And you won't let me make a good-luck charm for the business, or do an Incantation of Good Fortune, or even make a potion for your tomatoes . . ."

At that, Mr. Haggerthwaite went even redder. In fact, he began to look a little like a tomato himself. "Now look here, Mel!" he yelled. "That's enough! I've been growing tomatoes for years, and never a word of complaint from anyone. And as for this idea of yours . . . it's downright silly! Who do you think is going to hire you, for a start?"

"Plenty of people."

"What? In Bellstone? Bellstone's a traditional town. It doesn't go in for newfangled nonsense."

"We witches are traditional, too, I'll have you know. There've been witches for thousands of years! And lots of people have problems they need help sorting out. Problem relatives for instance . . . or problem husbands!"

"And what if that's true?" said Mr. Haggerthwaite, ignoring the jibe. "Say someone has a bad-tempered old granny, and they ask you to turn her into a bat. Well, either you don't—in which case there's no money for you. Or you do . . ."—Jessica and Nat could not help giggling—"in which case you'll have the police at your door. You can't turn people into bats."

"Don't be ridiculous, Tom," said Mrs. Haggerthwaite. "You know I don't do that kind of magic. Anyway, I've made up my mind. I am going to be a professional witch."

"Well, I've made up my mind that you won't!"

Jessica groaned. It was years since she and Nat had behaved like this. Anybody would think her parents were five-year-olds. She had a feeling that Nat was looking at her, no doubt with "I told you so" on his face, but she refused to meet his eyes.

"There's nothing you can do about it!" Mrs. Haggerthwaite crowed.

"Oh yes, there is!" her husband replied.

"Like what?" Mrs. Haggerthwaite jeered.

Mr. Haggerthwaite tried desperately to think of something. Mrs. Haggerthwaite was already smiling triumphantly, and it infuriated him. "I won't talk to you!" he yelled. "And I won't give you a foot rub when you're watching television!"

Mrs. Haggerthwaite laughed and it infuriated him still further.

"I won't live here anymore! I'll go and stay with Kate!" And this time it was Mr. Haggerthwaite who smiled triumphantly. He was sure, now, that he had won.

Nat could have told him otherwise. Nat could have pointed out that Mrs. Haggerthwaite was one of the most stubborn creatures on the planet. And you could never successfully call her bluff, ever.

"Good! You do that!" Mrs. Haggerthwaite yelled.

# Chapter Three

Later that day, Jessica sat on her bed. She was copying bits from *Astrophysics Made Simple* into a large red notebook. She did not know why, but somehow she could not concentrate.

"I hope you're pleased with yourself!"

Jessica looked up to see Nat glaring at her from the doorway.

"I don't know what you're talking about."

"Oh yes, you do. Thanks to you, Dad's walked out. What if he never comes back? We'll be a single-parent family."

Jessica swallowed. "There's nothing wrong with single-parent families," she said. "Lots of kids at school have them."

"As if that makes it better," said Nat fiercely.

"Anyway, other kids' single parents aren't Mom. Imagine, there'll be nothing to eat except nettle soup ever again!" (Jessica turned pale. It was a truly terrible thought.) "Besides," Nat added passionately, "I want Dad back."

"Perhaps we should learn to cook," said Jessica. But she knew it was not the answer. She was missing Mr. Haggerthwaite, too. When she remembered that he wasn't there, she felt all funny inside. And he had only been gone for two hours.

The truth was, she relied on him. Of course Mrs. Haggerthwaite could be lots of fun. Even Jessica had to admit that. Sometimes she even made eating nettle soup seem like fun. And even the time she had celebrated the Rites of Spring by dancing about on the roof wearing nothing but pink underwear had been quite funny . . . afterward. Moreover, she could be horribly rude to people she didn't like—which was funny when it was somebody Jessica didn't like either, though less funny when it was somebody she did. And she was loyal, too, like the time she had put a curse on Mr. Boswell, three doors down, because Nat had kicked his new football over the fence and Mr. Boswell wouldn't give it back. In fact, Mrs. Haggerthwaite had several good qualities.

But she was not very good at seeing other

people's point of view. Today, for example, she had not understood why everybody hated her new idea. Just as she never understood why Jessica minded when she filled the fridge with revolting ingredients for her spells, or when she borrowed Jessica's test tubes to use for her potions, or when she went to the school concert in a purple cape with magic runes all over it and all the kids stared.

Mr. Haggerthwaite, on the other hand, was very good at understanding people's feelings. He even managed to understand how Mrs. Haggerthwaite felt most of the time, which was fairly amazing. Certainly, he understood how Jessica felt. It was he, for example, who made sure that she had a sensible jacket to wear to school, one without magic runes. It was he who decided to take over most of the cooking, when Jessica was only five, after she hurled her nettle soup to the floor, breaking the bowl into a hundred pieces. It was he who took Jessica to the Natural History Museum over the holidays, and watched the science programs on TV with her without making rude remarks or saying "Science—fiddlesticks!" every two minutes.

And on Jessica's eleventh birthday, only last month, he had made sure that her present had been just what she had always wanted.

"I know what Jessica wants," she had overheard him saying to her mother. "Just you leave it to me."

"I don't believe you," Mrs. Haggerthwaite had replied. "It's so dull! It's so boring! I'm sure my idea is better."

"Not for Jessica," said Mr. Haggerthwaite. "Just trust me."

They had continued like this for some time, with Jessica desperately trying to work out what they were discussing. And then they had caught her listening and both been cross with her, and she had to give up. But for her birthday there had been exactly what she had always dreamed of but never thought she could possibly own: her own microscope. It was sitting on her desk now, just as shiny and wonderful as when she had first unwrapped it. Even looking at it made Jessica feel warm inside. "We can always take it back, you know," Mrs. Haggerthwaite had said hopefully. It turned out that Mrs. Haggerthwaite had wanted to give her a crystal ball.

Maybe I don't just rely on him, thought Jessica. Maybe I love him. After all, she thought defiantly, he is my dad.

"Don't worry," she said aloud to Nat. "They'll make up. They always do."

"Huh! I'm not so sure. Mom is the most stubborn person ever. And Dad's really mad this time, too." Nat was looking worried. "Maybe he won't come back for ages. Maybe he won't come back ever!"

"Of course he will! Don't worry about it," said Jessica authoritatively. "I'll sort it out."

Nat looked even more alarmed, if that were possible. "How are you going to do that?"

"I don't know," Jessica admitted. "But I'm sure the first thing is to stop this professional-witch business. Once Mom comes to her senses, Dad's sure to come home."

"She won't give up easily, that's certain," said Nat gloomily. "She's too stubborn. They both are. Neither of them wants to back down." Nat had a nasty feeling that Jessica was becoming headstrong again. "I think Mom is absolutely determined to be a professional witch."

"Yes, but *I* am absolutely determined that she won't."

Nat looked at Jessica, whose lips had set in a firm line. At that moment she looked horribly like Mrs. Haggerthwaite. Her black hair was shorter and wavier, and her nose was smaller than Mrs. Haggerthwaite's beak, and her eyes were brown not green—but they had exactly the same determined glitter.

Before he could say anything, they heard Mrs. Haggerthwaite calling them to come and eat. At exactly the same moment the same smell hit both their noses. They looked at each other in horror.

"Nettle soup!"

As soon as she could after dinner, Jessica escaped upstairs. She flung herself on her bed and opened up the red notebook. Then she ripped out all the notes she had made from *Astrophysics Made Simple*, and wrote PLAN OF ACTION in red capital letters on the first page.

She would soon sort things out, she thought hopefully, chewing on her pen. Nat was far too young to understand these things. He was only nine, and so it was quite natural (thought Jessica kindly)

that he should be alarmed. And in some ways she did not blame him: with parents as pig-headed as theirs, there was no telling what kind of mess they might get into. But she, Jessica, with two more years of wisdom and experience, knew how to cope with their parents' tantrums. She would make sure that this stupid squabble was soon forgotten. Then everything would be back to normal in no time.

The first thing was to stop her mother. She scowled.

Somehow thinking of an actual plan was more difficult than she had expected. She chewed her pen for a while. Then she closed her notebook. She wrote on the cover *Master Plan of Jessica*—and then she hesitated. *Jessica the Witch Hunter*, she thought, but that didn't sound quite right. *Jessica the Witch Terminator*? It sounded formidable, but perhaps a bit too fierce. She wasn't about to stick her mother on a bonfire, after all. Then it came to her. She wrote it down on the cover of her notebook.

Now she really had to think of a plan. She gazed absently around her bedroom at her microscope, her posters of the solar system and the one showing a skeleton of Tyrannosaurus Rex. Her eyes passed over her *Junior Science Encyclopedia* and the interesting fossil that she had found last summer on the beach, which she thought might be a prehistoric fish. (Nat thought it looked more like a prehistoric tadpole.)

And then it came to her. Of course. Science! Science was the enemy of witchcraft, if anything was. No scientist believed in magic.

Jessica wrote Plan A—Science. She added a few more notes. Then she snapped the notebook shut.

Just before she went to bed, she took out a large sheet of paper from her school science folder. On it she wrote, in huge, red capital letters, the same thing she had written on the cover of her notebook. She got up and stuck the paper to the outside of her bedroom door.

## JESSICA HAGGERTHWAITE
## WITCH DISPATCHER

That'll show her, she thought. Then she grinned. There was no doubt about it. She was going to enjoy being a witch dispatcher.

# Chapter Four

A t school the next day, Jessica found it hard to concentrate.

Usually she enjoyed school. Of course, sometimes her mind wandered, especially during Assembly and almost always during geography. But she paid attention during science and math, even if it was only long division. She had to, if she was going to be a famous scientist one day.

But today, even during science, she could not concentrate. And so it was that she almost missed Miss Barnaby's Big Announcement.

"Guess what, everybody! We are going to have a science competition!"

Most people ignored her. After all, it was almost time to go home. But Jessica sat up in her seat. She listened hard as Miss Barnaby explained that she would give everyone a topic, and they could then choose and design their own individual science project. They would carry it out on their own time and write up the results. There would be a display of the best projects and a prize for the winner.

A low grumbling began. Most of the class, it was clear, had no wish to spend their spare time on science. Only Jessica hugged herself under the desk. She could hardly wait to begin. She would do something on the ozone layer, or astrophysics, or dinosaurs. She had still not made up her mind when Miss Barnaby approached and told her she was to do a project on plants.

"But I don't want to do plants!" Jessica protested. "Can't I do black holes or asteroids?"

"Plants," said Miss Barnaby firmly, "are interesting, too. Besides you are down for plants on the list." She showed Jessica her name on a piece of paper, with *Plants* scrawled next to it. Jessica was not impressed with bits of paper, and saw no reason why "asteroids" could not be scrawled there instead. She made a face.

"Anyway, I can't do plants. My dad's a gardener. It wouldn't be fair."

"Nonsense," said Miss Barnaby. "We encourage parents to take an interest in projects." Then she

caught sight of Jessica's face, and suddenly remembered something urgent she had to do on the other side of the classroom. She could tell that Jessica was going to argue, and Miss Barnaby had found that when Jessica chose to argue, she, Miss Barnaby, usually ended up on the losing side.

Jessica was thinking of going after her when she was distracted by Robbie Flotsam, smirking at her across the desk.

"Hah! Got plants, did you, Jessie? Pretty flowers are just right for a girl."

"I'll still do better than you," Jessica shot back. She hated being called Jessie. "What did you get?"

Robbie looked uncomfortable.

"Computers."

"Computers!" Jessica crowed. "Computers!"

It was well known that Robbie Flotsam was hopeless with computers. He was new last year and before that, it seemed, had never touched a computer in his life. For that matter, he seemed to be hopeless at most things, with the exception of shoving other kids' heads through the railings so that they got stuck. He was very good at that.

"Better than silly old flowers!" he jeered.

"We'll see," said Jessica.

She was so busy thinking about the science competition that she almost forgot about Plan A.

But when the bell rang and everyone else had filed out, she went to the front of the class and stood by Miss Barnaby's desk. Miss Barnaby looked up in surprise.

"Hello there, Jessica. What can I do for you?" A rather nervous expression crossed her face. "It isn't about your science project?"

"No," said Jessica. "It's about my mom."

"Oh." Miss Barnaby looked relieved, even pleased. She was always hoping that her pupils would confide their home problems, but so far they never had.

Jessica took a deep breath. "Miss Barnaby. Have you heard that my mother is a witch?"

This was not the sort of home problem Miss Barnaby had been trained to deal with. She went a little pink. "Now, Jessica, don't be silly. You know there are no such things as witches."

"I know that, but my mom doesn't. She thinks she is one."

"Oh, dear! I mean, I know she's eccentric . . ."

"No, she really believes it. She wants to go professional. And I think somebody should talk to her and tell her what a stupid idea it is."

Miss Barnaby looked hot and bothered. "Perhaps you're right. Maybe you should get a relative to talk to her, somebody she respects . . ."

"Miss Barnaby," said Jessica firmly, "I want *you* to talk to her."

"Oh, dear! No, I don't think I could do that! I mean, it's none of my business what your mother does on her own time."

"Miss Barnaby," said Jessica, "you're a *scientist*. You know that witches don't exist. I mean, if anything is against witchcraft, it's science. You're the perfect person to tell Mom."

Miss Barnaby gazed at Jessica worriedly. Perhaps she was wondering whether studying a little bi-

ology at college really qualified her to instruct Mrs. Haggerthwaite on the lack of a scientific basis for witchcraft. Or perhaps she was just frightened of Mrs. Haggerthwaite: a lot of people were. After all, even if you knew she could not really be a witch, she still looked like one, with her big nose and her long black hair, and she certainly *acted* like one.

Then again, if Mrs. Haggerthwaite was intimidating, so was her daughter. So Miss Barnaby was only a little surprised when she found herself agreeing to Jessica's plans.

"Good," said Jessica. "Don't be late."

And she ran off to find Nat, leaving a stunned Miss Barnaby behind her.


Jessica found Nat sitting by the fence, looking hunched and miserable. Robbie Flotsam was there, too, but at least he was not shoving Nat's head through the railings. Instead he was swinging from them by his hands and feet.

"They're all crazy in your family," he was sneering as Jessica came up behind him. "Your sister's mad—she thinks she's going to be a scientist. As if! She's only a girl. And your mom's loony! Look at her at the school concert, wearing that purple dress! And carrying that frog around! And now she's telling everyone she's a witch . . ."

Jessica waited until Robbie was suspended from one hand only. Then she clobbered him hard in the back with her schoolbag. With a yell Robbie hit the ground. Jessica was pleased to see that he landed in a large puddle.

"Just you leave my brother alone! And how do you know our mom's a witch? I mean," she corrected herself quickly, "who said she was one?"

Robbie aimed a swipe at Jessica's ankles, but she dodged easily. He sat up and rubbed his head, scowling. "*She* did, stupid! She called up yesterday

and told the paper. She wants to put an advertisement in for customers, but my dad won't let her."

Jessica felt a shiver pass down her back. Mom wanted to put an ad in the paper! *Thank goodness* Jessica was putting Plan A into action and stopping all this nonsense. Out loud she said, "What's your dad got to do with it? I thought he owned a hotel."

"*Three* hotels. But he owns the *Bellstone Gazette*, too. He's a very important businessman," said Robbie smugly. "And he said there's no way he's

putting your mom's advertisement in the paper. He said it would bring the *Gazette* into disrepute."

Robbie looked very pleased with himself, but Jessica, who knew plenty of long words of her own, was not impressed. "Huh! Well, you can tell him from me—" And then she stopped short, because for once she could think of nothing to say. After all, it was not as if she *wanted* Mr. Flotsam to put an ad in his paper: In fact, it was the *last* thing she wanted. So she just said, "Come on, Nat! We have important things to do."

And she dragged Nat off, leaving Robbie staring after them.

# Chapter Five

Meanwhile, Mrs. Haggerthwaite was not having a good day.

First the *Bellstone Gazette* had called to say that after talking to their owner, Mr. Flotsam himself, they had decided not to publish her advertisement. This was bad enough. Then came her interview with the bank manager.

Mrs. Haggerthwaite had been looking forward to this. She was sure that once the bank understood the wonderful opportunity that she was presenting, they would be falling over themselves to offer her money. Money that she could use to rent an office in which to see clients. Money that she could use to advertise her new business, too. If the *Bellstone Gazette* would not help, then she would give Bellstone Local Radio a try. She had even thought of a jingle.

*For spells that work without a hitch*
*call Mellandra Haggerthwaite,*
*Professional Witch!*

Mr. Humbert, the bank manager, was short and plump with an irritable expression and eyes that reminded her of Liverwort. They bulged and stared, and they bulged and stared all the more when he finally understood what Mrs. Haggerthwaite wanted.

"But Mrs. . . ."—he checked his notes—"Mrs. Haggerthwaite, let me get this straight. You are actually asking this bank to lend you a fairly substantial sum of money in order that you can go into business as . . . as a witch?"

"Exactly," said Mrs. Haggerthwaite through clenched teeth. She thought Mr. Humbert was not very bright. After all, she had spent the last ten minutes explaining this.

"But that's preposterous!"

Mrs. Haggerthwaite bristled.

"It's not preposterous at all! I've already explained. I'm a witch of long standing, but I never thought of going professional before. Then I realized what a wonderful opportunity it is. You see, there just aren't any other witches in Bellstone."

"I'm well aware of that," said Mr. Humbert nastily. "None that we're lending money to, anyway."

"The point is," Mrs. Haggerthwaite snapped, "that no other witches means there's no competition."

"There's no competition for fairy godmothers either. Or frog princes. But I wouldn't give money to them."

Mrs. Haggerthwaite scowled. "You think this is funny, don't you?"

"Not at all. I never find the idea of throwing money away funny." Mr. Humbert ignored Mrs. Haggerthwaite bristling at him across the desk. He added thoughtfully, "You know, I don't think I've heard anything quite so ridiculous since the person who wanted to set up an import business in spotted toads. I mean . . . toads!"

"I've got a toad," said Mrs. Haggerthwaite coldly. "And he's spotty."

To prove her point she produced Liverwort, who had been nestling quite happily in her coat pocket, and put him down on Mr. Humbert's desk. Mr. Humbert stared at Liverwort as if he could not believe his eyes. And a moment later, despite all her protests, Mrs. Haggerthwaite found herself and her toad back out on the street.

But Mrs. Haggerthwaite was nothing if not determined. She decided to try her luck with the Small Business Adviser who worked for the Town Council giving grants to "new entrepreneurs with potential." Mrs. Haggerthwaite was convinced she had plenty of potential.

And certainly the Small Business Adviser was much nicer than Mr. Humbert. "Goodness," she murmured, "a professional witch! That's a new one. I suppose it would be a personal service, wouldn't it, rather than a manufacturing facility?"

"Yes," said Mrs. Haggerthwaite. "It would. Of course I do manufacture the potions and powders I use, but I'm not intending to sell them in bulk."

"A personal service then," said the Adviser. She opened a file. "Let's see. We have hairdressers and massage therapists and travel agents and manicurists. That's not really you, though, is it?"

"No," Mrs. Haggerthwaite admitted.

"We have home nurses and midwives. Is that the sort of thing?"

"Not really. I mean, I do healing potions but I'm not a doctor. It's more a matter of healing people who are under a curse, that sort of thing."

"I see." The Adviser swallowed.

"Although a posset of nettles and comfrey is very helpful against colds. Actually it's meant to ward off vampires, but I find it works equally well for both."

"I see," said the Adviser again. She was beginning to look a little nervous. "So you don't really fit with the acupuncturist either?"

"No," said Mrs. Haggerthwaite cheerfully. "I don't

stick pins into people. Just into their wax images. It feels to them like red-hot pokers!"

The Adviser turned pale and began to shuffle her papers together in a fidgety way.

"I'm only joking!" said Mrs. Haggerthwaite hastily. "I never do black magic! I wouldn't dream of it."

"I see," said the Adviser. She did not look entirely reassured. "Well, I would like to help you, I really would, but I've never heard anything quite like your case before. And I'm afraid we have very strict guidelines for giving out grants. It has to be an approved business. I just don't think witchcraft counts. I'm sorry, really I am."

"So am I," said Mrs. Haggerthwaite.

As she walked home, she could not help feeling a bit depressed. It was raining, and the water was running down the back of her collar and creeping up through the holes in her boots. For the first time, Mrs. Haggerthwaite wondered whether she was doing the right thing. It occurred to her that nobody was on her side. Mrs. Haggerthwaite was not a person who cared greatly what the world thought of her, but she had never before felt that absolutely everybody was lined up against her, even her husband and her children.

She paused under a shop awning. She thought

about the fact that it was nettle soup for dinner again.

And she very nearly abandoned her plan.

But then her pride kicked in. "Bank managers!" she sniffed. "Who needs them! I can run my business from home. As for advertisements—I'll make my own!"

She set off into the rain with a new spring in her step.

When Jessica and Nat arrived home, it was to find their mother scribbling away at a new list. Next to her, on the kitchen table, was a large pile of paper with Liverwort perched on top of it as a paperweight.

"So how is the witch business going?" asked Jessica. "Did you get lots of customers today?"

"I didn't get any customers," said Mrs. Haggerthwaite coldly. "I didn't expect to. It takes a while to build up business."

"I expect it does. Especially," added Jessica nastily, "when you can't even advertise in the paper."

"I don't need the stupid *Bellstone Gazette!*" Mrs. Haggerthwaite swept up Liverwort (who croaked reproachfully) and waved a piece of paper at Jessica. "Look at this! I made it myself."

Jessica looked and her heart sank. It was a poster with a big picture of Mrs. Haggerthwaite, one which Mr. Haggerthwaite had taken last Christmas.

In it she wore dangly earrings and her favorite blouse—the one with shiny moons and stars all over it—and she had her lucky amulet around her neck. Her big nose was much in evidence, and her big teeth, and she looked very witchlike. Across the top was written *Mellandra Haggerthwaite, Professional Witch* in spiky letters. Below that it said *consultations, charms, spells, predictions, escryings, gramarye and curse-breaking* followed by their own address and telephone number.

"I got the idea from your posters," said Mrs. Haggerthwaite nastily.

Jessica swallowed. There was no doubt about it, once this got around Bellstone, life would not be worth living.

"I'm going to put them up all over town!" said Mrs. Haggerthwaite, adding to her misery. "I've had a hundred of them printed in that shop at the corner. By the end of the week there won't be a single person in Bellstone who hasn't heard of Mellandra Haggerthwaite, Professional Witch!"

Jessica was still struggling for a reply when the doorbell rang. So she went to answer the door instead.

It was Miss Barnaby. She was looking rather nervous—not at all like the stern and remorseless scientist that Jessica had hoped for. And when she stepped into the kitchen and saw Mrs. Haggerthwaite . . . well, she looked positively frightened.

"Ah, Mrs. Haggerthwaite . . . so sorry to disturb you. I should have phoned first, I know. It's just that I've been hearing things about your, er, new line of business, and I was hoping we could have a little chat . . ."

Mrs. Haggerthwaite jumped up and flung out a welcoming hand. It turned out to have Liverwort still in it, and Miss Barnaby leaped back with a shriek.

"I'm delighted to see you," said Mrs. Haggerthwaite, dumping Liverwort quickly on the table. "How wonderful that my very first customer should be Jessica's teacher!"

Miss Barnaby was horrified.

"Oh, well, actually, that wasn't . . . at least, I did want to talk to you about witchcraft but . . ."

"No need to be shy! Just tell me what I can do for you. A philter, a potion, a look into the future? Perhaps you are under a curse? Or you have a bad case of warts?"

Miss Barnaby jumped, then blushed. "How did you know about the warts?"

"Mom!" said Jessica firmly. "You don't understand. Miss Barnaby isn't a customer . . ."

"Now, Jessica," interrupted Mrs. Haggerthwaite. "Why don't you and Nat go upstairs? Miss Barnaby and I have things to discuss." Her hand gripped Jessica's shoulder firmly as she shoved her toward the door.

"You tell her!" Jessica looked at Miss Barnaby for help. But to her astonishment, her teacher would not meet her eyes.

"Actually, dear, I think your mother and I would

get on better by ourselves. We'll have a little chat about the whole thing, looking at it from every angle . . ."

This was the last thing Jessica wanted. And if there had been only Miss Barnaby to contend with, she would have had her way. But, as Nat could have warned her, there was one person who was every bit as stubborn and determined and pig-headed and downright obstinate as Jessica herself. That person was Mrs. Haggerthwaite.

To her huge annoyance, Jessica found herself on the other side of the kitchen door.

There was nothing else to do, so Jessica stomped off to see her father. He was weeding Aunt Kate's vegetable patch, but perfectly happy to stop and chat with his daughter. He was less happy when she lost no time in ordering him home.

It was true that Mr. Haggerthwaite was homesick. It was true that Aunt Kate would not let him cook, watch baseball on TV, or wear his heavy gardening boots in the house, and that he was beginning to feel bloated from too much cake. It was true that the spare bed had lumps in it. It was true that he was tired of Aunt Kate saying, "What a load of old hogwash, Tom Haggerthwaite! Your place is with your wife and kids!" It was true that he missed his children every bit as much as they missed him. And yet when Jessica coaxed and ordered and wheedled and even shouted at him, he just shook his head mulishly. Or else he shrugged and looked miserable.

"The fact is, your mom doesn't want me home," he said. "She's made that clear. She doesn't think I can earn a living. She doesn't think I deserve to be consulted about her plans. She doesn't even think I can grow tomatoes without her help!"

Jessica told him that she and Nat wanted him home, that they were sure he could make a living, that they would always consult him—and that they were happy to let him grow tomatoes his own way, too. But it did no good. Mr. Haggerthwaite was ready to walk Jessica all the way back to her front gate, but he would not step through it.

None of this made Jessica very happy. And it did not make her feel any better when she found Mrs. Haggerthwaite alone in the kitchen, bustling around with her herbs and potions, humming as she worked and clearly in a very good mood indeed.

"I really must thank you, Jessica, for telling Miss Barnaby about me. Thanks to you I have my very first client!"

Jessica gritted her teeth and said nothing.

Instead, while Mrs. Haggerthwaite was searching for something on the pantry shelves, she went to look at her mother's spell book, which was lying open on the table.

"You're making her a love potion?"

Mrs. Haggerthwaite jumped.

"Jessica! How dare you read my spell book! Matters like this are secret. We witches need to be discreet." She snatched the spell book away, then shoveled a sweet-smelling powder into a bowl. "Anyway, Miss Barnaby's ever so nice. Why shouldn't she have a nice boyfriend?"

"If she doesn't have a boyfriend, it's because she lacks gumption," Jessica declared. "And loyalty," she added.

"Nonsense! I think she's delightful. And she's just the customer I need. This could be only the beginning. Apparently her best friend needs some fortune-telling, and her sister could do with a good-luck charm for her driving test next week. Why, who knows where this might lead?"

Jessica groaned. Plan A had gone horribly wrong. And, like her mother, she had a feeling this was only the start.

That evening, Mrs. Haggerthwaite made them march for hours around the town, helping distribute

the posters. Jessica argued and Nat complained but Mrs. Haggerthwaite would not listen.

Nobody wanted Mrs. Haggerthwaite's posters. The library said they did not display hoax posters, which made Mrs. Haggerthwaite really cross. The supermarket said they did not want to offend their customers: After all, Bellstone was a traditional town. And as for the church bulletin board, the woman there looked as if she was going to explode when she understood what Mrs. Haggerthwaite was advertising.

"We'll have none of that here," she said fiercely. "And what the minister will say when she hears, I really don't like to think."

But, as Jessica had feared, Mrs. Haggerthwaite was nothing if not determined. She bought five packets of tea in the corner shop, and five bags of raisins in the health-food store, so they just had to put up her poster. She stopped asking in supermarkets, but slipped in when the assistants' backs were turned. She sent Nat into the library as an undercover agent, because he was too young for the librarians to get angry at him. And she pasted up posters in bus shelters, on the railings next to the town hall and on the boarded-up shop on the corner that was still waiting to be sold. Jessica had a sneaking feeling that this was probably illegal but, as

Mrs. Haggerthwaite pointed out, there were flyers up for rock concerts, so why not for witchcraft?

"Anyway, we witches don't worry about petty regulations," said Mrs. Haggerthwaite grandly. "Live dangerously, Jessica!"

Jessica scowled. She knew that she did not have much choice.

Before she went to bed that night, Jessica altered the sign on her door. It now read:

**JESSICA HAGGERTHWAITE**
**PROFESSIONAL WITCH DISPATCHER**
**All manner of witches dispatched with**
**scientific methods for modest fees**

"That'll show her," Jessica muttered to herself.

Then she opened her notebook and under Plan A wrote *Failed—Miss Barnaby was useless. Mom brainwashed her and she didn't even put up a fight.* Then, on a new page, she wrote *Plan B*. She sat for a while with her eyes shut, but no ideas came.

Never mind. She would sleep on it. In the morning, she was certain, Plan B would appear.

# Chapter Six

"I can't believe your mom thinks she's a witch. I mean, does she believe it or is she just trying to pull a fast one to make some money? If so, it's a cheap trick, my dad says. But if she does think she's one, then she's crazy."

Jessica looked up from her notebook and scowled. She was not thrilled that Robbie Flotsam had taken the trouble to come over to share his opinions with her, although it was more than could be said for the rest of her class. She was uncomfortably aware that her best friend, Clare (at least she had been her best friend), was on the other side of the playground, giggling away with a group of girls that Jessica did not like at all. They had not said outright that Jessica could not join them. But she had caught several remarks along the lines of "thinks she's a witch, you know" and "out of her mind, that's what my mom says" when they knew Jessica was listening. So she had decided she would rather sit and write in her notebook instead.

Maybe Clare was a bit put out that Jessica had hardly seen her recently. But that was not Jessica's fault! Since her father moved out and her mother started this witch nonsense (yes, it always came back to that), neither of them had seemed to have time to take Jessica over to Clare's house any more. But surely a best friend should understand these things? Surely a best friend should not go off with other people?

Jessica dragged her attention back to Robbie Flotsam, who was grinning at her in a particularly infuriating manner. "Your mom's crazy!" he said, just in case she had missed the point.

"Often great geniuses are thought to be mad," Jessica told him coldly.

"What, you think she's a genius?"

Jessica, of course, thought no such thing. She hesitated. Robbie pressed on.

"Well, my dad says she's a disgrace, and if she doesn't watch out, he's going to publish an article telling everyone what a disgrace she is."

"What are you talking about?"

"Just what I said! It will finish her business for good, he says. It's going to be in the *Gazette* and everyone will read it."

Robbie looked so smug that Jessica would normally have been provoked, but now her mind was busy working on what he had told her.

"Can he really do that?"

"Of course he can. He can publish what he likes. Mind you, I'm not sure your mom's important enough to be in an article—Hey! Get off!" For

Jessica, gripped by a new idea, had leaped up and started shaking him, shouting, "She *is* important enough! She *is*!"

"You're crazy, too!" Robbie yelled, backing away.

Jessica swallowed and counted to ten.

"Look," she said, as calmly as possible, "can I come over and talk to your dad?"

"Why? He's not going to take any notice of you. Anyway, he's busy—important people are." And Robbie tried to look important himself.

Jessica could see that desperate measures were needed. Before she had really thought about it, she said, "I'll help you with your science project."

Robbie went very red. "I don't need your help!"

"Yes, you do! You're terrible at science."

Robbie looked ready to explode. With a huge effort, Jessica tried to be tactful. "All right, you're not terrible at science. But you know you're no good with computers. If I just helped you a bit, well, then you'd probably win."

She certainly hoped not. She was not sure that anything, even witch dispatching, was worth the humiliation of being beaten in a science competition by Robbie Flotsam. But she tried not to think about this.

There was a brief pause while Robbie struggled with her suggestion.

"All right," he said at last. "You can come over after school."

Jessica beamed at him. She knew she had found Plan B.

It felt very strange indeed to go home with Robbie Flotsam, and Jessica did her best to ignore the nudges and giggles as they walked together out of the school gate. But she soon forgot about school. The Flotsams lived on the other side of Bellstone, in one of Mr. Flotsam's hotels. It was a very grand building, standing in acres of gardens. Despite herself, Jessica was impressed.

They found Mr. Flotsam sitting behind a vast desk in a room full of wood paneling and gold-framed pictures.

"Jessica Haggerthwaite," Mr. Flotsam repeated, after Robbie had introduced her. "That sounds familiar."

"I'm in the same class as Robbie," said Jessica, although she thought that as Mr. Flotsam had never bothered to come to the school, not to the craft show or the concert (he was always too busy, Robbie said), he was unlikely to have heard of her.

"No, no. I know what it is! Tom Haggerthwaite. An exceptionally talented garden designer. I was speaking to him only this morning."

Jessica glowed.

"That's my dad. Does that mean you'll be giving him the contract for your hotels?" she asked. She had forgotten until now about the big gardening contract her father had mentioned.

"We'll have to see," said Mr. Flotsam, winking. "A good businessman never says yes right away! I need to see what I can get out of your dad first." Jessica was thinking this sounded rather mean, but then Mr. Flotsam continued, "It would be wonderful for him, of course. It's a huge contract. And I'd recommend him to all the businessmen who stay in my hotel. It would guarantee his success."

"Oh, please give him the contract! Please!"

"We'll see," said Mr. Flotsam. "He didn't send you here to beg, did he?"

"Of course not! Actually, I came over to work on Robbie's science project with him."

"Humph," said Mr. Flotsam. "That sounds like a thankless task." Even Jessica, who had hated Robbie from the first time she met him, thought this remark was pretty unkind.

"By the way, about my mom," said Jessica hastily.

"She's Mellandra Haggerthwaite, the professional witch, you know. Robbie told me you were thinking of putting an article about her in your paper."

"Oh, yes. And what if I am?"

"Well, I think you should."

"You do?" Mr. Flotsam looked surprised.

"Oh, yes," said Jessica. And she started pointing out what a good story it would make. After all, Mrs. Haggerthwaite was the first witch in Bellstone for hundreds of years, probably. And before she knew it, Jessica was telling him all about her mother's spells and Liverwort and the bank manager and the posters and Miss Barnaby. And that in the week since then there had been a steady stream of customers, starting with friends of Miss Barnaby and going on to their friends and friends of their friends.

"Hmm," said Mr. Flotsam when she had finished. "I think you're right. It would make a good story. I wonder, will your mother be home this evening?"

Jessica nodded.

"Well, then. How about if you have a bite to eat with us? Then I can run you home afterward and have a word with your mother at the same time."

Jessica agreed eagerly. And Robbie, much to her surprise, grinned and gave her a wink. She was so surprised she almost winked back.

They ate in the hotel dining room, which Jessica found very grand. Robbie said they did it all the time. While they ate, Mr. Flotsam talked to Jessica, asking her lots of questions about school and science and witchcraft, and almost totally ignoring Robbie, even when he tried to talk about his own science project. Jessica wondered whether Mrs. Flotsam paid any more attention to her son than Mr. Flotsam did. Then she remembered that someone had said that Robbie's mother had gone to live in Canada. At the time she had thought this perfectly understandable, but now she wondered how she would feel being left with only Mr. Flotsam for a parent.

In the car, Mr. Flotsam kept chattering on about how much he liked Jessica's idea for an article. Even though she did not like Mr. Flotsam, Jessica could not help feeling rather smug about all the praise she was getting. And for a while she was so busy feeling smug that she did not listen that hard to what Mr. Flotsam was actually saying.

"Of course, when I first heard about your mother, I thought, this is a lot of nonsense! We can't have a witch in Bellstone, Bert, I said to myself, it will give Bellstone a Bad Name. And that will be the worst possible thing for business. But then several of the guests in the hotel started asking for her. Yes, the receptionist had to find out her number for people who wanted consultations. And everybody's talking about her! And then, when you came by, I thought, maybe the whole thing's quite a good idea! Why, I wouldn't be surprised if she doesn't become a tourist attraction. And that will be the best possible thing for business!"

Jessica had a nasty feeling, like cold water trickling down her back. "So what kind of article are you going to publish?" she asked.

"Oh, a fun feature, I thought! Something bright and cheerful! We'll have a big picture of her, and perhaps one of that toad you were telling me about. And a bit about how she got started. And then a few fun spells for everyone to try at home. She could even have a weekly column! Magic with Mellandra, something like that."

"But Mr. Flotsam, I thought you were going to say witches were a bad thing."

"Oh, goodness me, no! You don't think I'd do something like that to the mother of Robbie's friend, now do you?"

Jessica had a horrible feeling in the pit of her stomach. Robbie, realizing that something was wrong, gave her such a sympathetic look that Jessica bit off the comment she had been about to make, that if being friends with Robbie was the problem, she could easily fix that. Still, she really didn't see why someone who could be so mean to his own son couldn't be mean to the mother of one of his friends, too.

# Chapter Seven

If Nat was surprised when Jessica told him that she was going home with Robbie Flotsam, he did not say anything. And he soon forgot all about it. For when he arrived home it was to find Mr. Haggerthwaite balanced on top of a stepladder in the living room.

"Dad!" Nat yelled. In his enthusiasm he grabbed the bottom of the ladder, which began to shake.

"Hey, watch it," said Mr. Haggerthwaite, but he was grinning.

"Have you come home to stay?"

"Oh, no," said Mr. Haggerthwaite quickly. "I'm just doing a little decorating, that's all. Your mother asked me to help out."

He waved the lengths of black and purple cloth that he was busy hanging from the ceiling. Even though he had not made up with Mrs. Haggerthwaite, he was thrilled to be home—if only for an evening. Nat was thrilled, too. They were both so happy that they did not stop to wonder why Mrs. Haggerthwaite wanted huge pieces of purple cloth draped around the living room.

"And afterward," Mr. Haggerthwaite added, "I'm going to stay and watch the game on television. Your mom said I could. It's the big game tonight and Kate doesn't like baseball. We can watch together!"

Nat beamed. He said hopefully, "Maybe you could cook dinner, too?"

"Of course I could! Chicken, macaroni and cheese—whatever you like! Or baked potatoes—they're still Jessica's favorite?"

Nat was just explaining that Jessica was at a friend's house when they heard the front door slam. A moment later Mrs. Haggerthwaite was standing in the doorway. Her arms held a whole jumble of objects: trails of ivy, twigs from the garden, candles, and something that looked suspiciously like a skull (only, thought Nat quickly, it couldn't possibly be).

"Hello, Nat," she said. "Isn't it nice? We're going

to have a lovely new living room! After all, I can't have consultations in a room that looks like this. I mean nobody thinks of a witch surrounded by pink cushions and frilly lampshades. Do they?"

"No," said Nat. He thought that most people didn't think of witches living in Bellstone at all, but in dark caves with bats and cobwebs or in ruined towers in the middle of forests. He also thought his mother might have asked Jessica and him before she decided to change the living room around. But he decided not to say anything. He was too happy that his father was home. And anyway, like Jessica, he realized that his mother was not always good at understanding other people's feelings. She probably thought that just because she would like the living room draped in purple and with twigs dropping on her head, then everybody else would, too.

He was a bit surprised that his father said nothing. After all, Mr. Haggerthwaite was meant to be dead set against this witch business. But he just went on whistling cheerfully as he hammered nails into the ceiling. So Nat joined in, too. He helped Mrs. Haggerthwaite cover the shelves and furniture with bits of moss and twigs, and he pinned trails of ivy to the curtains. By the time they had finished, it really did look like a witch's cavern.

"The game will be on soon, Tom," said Mrs. Haggerthwaite when they had finished admiring the effect.

"Oh, there's a while yet," said Mr. Haggerthwaite. "Why don't I rustle us up something to eat before the game starts?"

"There's no need for that. I can always heat up some nettle soup." But even Mrs. Haggerthwaite was tired of nettle soup. And from the loud groan, it was clear enough that Nat was. "On second thought . . . that would be nice."

So Mr. Haggerthwaite went to have a look in the cupboards. Mrs. Haggerthwaite and Nat set the table, but after that they just sat and chatted with Mr. Haggerthwaite. It was true that Nat chatted more than Mrs. Haggerthwaite did. But then again, even she had more to say than Liverwort, who just sat on Nat's knee and burped.

"You're in a very cheerful mood, Tom," Mrs. Haggerthwaite observed after a while. Mr. Haggerthwaite was whistling, and he had just begun to fry some onions so that a lovely, sizzling fried-onion smell was filling the room.

"I suppose I am. Kate never lets me near a frying pan. I must miss it."

"Well, you can cook for us any time," said Mrs. Haggerthwaite. Then she went a little pink, as if she just realized what she had said, and she rushed on quickly before anyone could say anything, "So how is business? I've been meaning to ask."

"Well, I may have some good news there," said Mr. Haggerthwaite. He was looking a little pink, too, although it might have been the heat from the onions. "I went to see Bert Flotsam this morning. You know he owns all those big hotels. Well, he

does want his properties landscaped. And I think he may give the job to me!"

"Why, that's wonderful, Tom!" said Mrs. Haggerthwaite. She actually sounded as if she meant it.

"And how about you, Mel? I've been hearing all kinds of things about this witching business of yours. Why, everyone's talking about it—and most folks are impressed. Even Bert Flotsam had a good word."

"Well, it's early yet, of course," said Mrs. Haggerthwaite modestly. "But I do seem to be getting some customers. I had six today!"

"That's great!" And Mr. Haggerthwaite sounded as if he meant it, too.

"Thank you, Tom. But I thought you didn't approve of my going professional? In fact, I thought you were dead set against the idea."

Mr. Haggerthwaite looked awkward. "Well, I am. Or rather, I was. I wondered if you knew what you were taking on. Bellstone is so set in its ways. But if you can show them—and make a go of it— then good for you, I say!"

Mrs. Haggerthwaite looked terribly pleased. Then everyone fell silent for a while, but it was a friendly silence and, on Mrs. Haggerthwaite's part, a thoughtful one.

Nat squeezed his hands together with excitement. He could not believe that his parents were being so friendly toward each other. He wondered whether they actually missed each other, now that they were living apart. He wondered whether, if business was good and they found they did not need to worry about money quite so much, there might be less for them to fight about. He wondered whether his father was going to come home for good.

Then he crossed his fingers under the table and hoped and prayed that Jessica would not return too soon. She was sure to rush in and spoil things if she did.

It was a wonderful evening. Mr. Haggerthwaite served sausages and fried onions with gravy and lovely, creamy, mashed potatoes. There was a salad of homegrown tomatoes on the side, because Mr. Haggerthwaite did not consider a meal to be a meal without some of his homegrown vegetables. The tomatoes were an early variety and still rather green, but Mrs. Haggerthwaite and Nat assured him that the tartness complemented the spicy sausages beautifully. Then there were baked apples filled with bubbling jam and served with Mr. Haggerthwaite's pudding (which was perfectly smooth, unlike Mrs. Haggerthwaite's, which always had lumps in it).

They were just sighing with fullness and contentment when Mr. Haggerthwaite realized that the game would be coming on, and they all rushed into the living room.

Mr. Haggerthwaite's team won by three runs. The yell that he gave on the first almost took the ceiling off, and Liverwort immediately scuttled away under the sofa.

Nat was thrilled, because their team had not won much all season.

Mrs. Haggerthwaite was thrilled, because she had said a special Incantation of Good Fortune, and it had worked.

Mr. Haggerthwaite was the most thrilled of all; in fact, he was so thrilled that he kissed Mrs. Haggerthwaite. Then he looked terribly surprised and went very red, and she looked very red, too, but they were both smiling.

And it was then that Jessica arrived.

As Mr. Haggerthwaite and Nat were still watching the highlights from the game, Mrs. Haggerthwaite invited Mr. Flotsam into the kitchen. Jessica, who was just as pleased as Nat to see her father back home again, badly wanted to go into the living room. But she did not feel that she should leave her mother and Mr. Flotsam to have their chat without her. So she sat down next to Robbie at the kitchen table and waited for Mrs. Haggerthwaite to burst into joy and excitement about all the free publicity she was going to receive.

At first it seemed that this might happen. As Mrs. Haggerthwaite listened to Mr. Flotsam, her eyes grew large as saucers. But then they began to glitter in the dangerous way that Jessica knew so well. With a suddenly leaping heart, Jessica realized that her mother was not pleased at all.

"I see," said Mrs. Haggerthwaite shortly when Mr. Flotsam had finished. "So what you want is a nasty, sensationalist little column! And a picture of me with a black hat and a broomstick, no doubt! And easy spells for readers to try at home! As if I would ever break my vows of secrecy in that way! Well, you can just think again! Because the answer's no!"

"Oh, come now," said Mr. Flotsam genially. "Think of the publicity! And as to the spells . . . why, I'm sure you have plenty of silly ones that we could use."

Of course Mrs. Haggerthwaite did not think any of her spells were silly. And as the discussion continued she grew more and more cross. The article was a rotten idea, she said, and Mr. Flotsam was rotten for suggesting it. In fact, in her opinion he was nothing but an ignorant, publicity-crazed buffoon.

At this, Mr. Flotsam grew red in the face. He started shouting at Mrs. Haggerthwaite, and in a moment they were hurling the most horrible insults at each other. Jessica and Robbie looked at each other, dismayed.

"You'll be sorry for this!" Mr. Flotsam yelled at last. "You—you—old witch!"

"Middle-aged!" Mrs. Haggerthwaite yelled. "But otherwise right!"

It was at this moment that Mr. Haggerthwaite came into the kitchen with Nat. Mr. Haggerthwaite looked very surprised indeed to see Mr. Flotsam sitting there.

"Why, hello, Bert," he said. But before he could say anything more, Mr. Flotsam had turned his angry face toward him.

"And as for you!" Mr. Flotsam shouted. "You are the last person I would ever allow near one of my hotels! You can just forget that contract! I am never doing business with a Haggerthwaite again!"

"I don't understand—" Mr. Haggerthwaite began, but it was too late. Mr. Flotsam had grabbed Robbie and stormed out of the house.

# Chapter Eight

Afterward, Jessica thought it was the most terrible fight her parents had ever had.

It was strange really, because they had had noisier fights, and longer fights, where they shouted more and called each other ruder names. This time they did not shout or call each other anything at all. But somehow that seemed almost worse. Jessica thought it might have something to do with the way her father looked. He seemed so terribly sad and hurt.

But at first he did not look either of those things. He just seemed dazed.

"What's been going on?" he asked, turning puzzled eyes toward his wife.

"What's been going on," said Mrs. Haggerthwaite,

"is that Bert Flotsam is an idiot and a buffoon! And I told him so as well!" And she related to Mr. Haggerthwaite exactly what had happened.

As he listened, Mr. Haggerthwaite went paler and paler. And all the time Jessica could feel Nat's eyes boring into her. You've done it again, they seemed to say. But she did not need to be told. She had a terrible feeling that once again everything had gone horribly wrong.

"But I don't understand," said Mr. Haggerthwaite at last. "Even if you didn't like the idea of an article, was there any need to be so rude?"

"Of course there was!" Mrs Haggerthwaite declared. "Why, it was the most preposterous thing I ever heard!"

"But what about my contract?" said Mr. Haggerthwaite quietly. "You heard what he said. Didn't you think of that?"

There was a terrible silence. Mrs. Haggerthwaite looked red, and then she looked white, but she did not seem to know what to say. Mr. Haggerthwaite stood very still for a moment. Then he turned and walked quietly out of the house.

Nat burst into tears. And Jessica knew that nothing could ever be so bad again.

For a full minute afterward Jessica was rooted to the floor.

She wanted to run after her father and hug him and bring him back, but somehow she couldn't move. At the same time, she wanted to shout at her mother. And yet she could tell that Mrs. Haggerthwaite felt bad, too. She just sat at the kitchen table with Liverwort on her lap and did not say a word. But when Nat began to cry, Jessica had no time for either of her parents. She was too concerned with Nat. He ran out of the kitchen, and she raced after him and up the stairs.

"Please, Nat! Don't cry. They're not worth it. They're the most useless pair of parents I ever met. They're the most bad-tempered, piggish, selfish, nasty . . ."

"Shut up!"

Nat had reached the top of the stairs and turned around. He was crimson in the face.

"They are not!" he yelled at her. "They're good parents! They just have stupid fights, that's all. And I want Dad back!"

"Oh." It was so unusual for Nat to shout at her, that for a moment Jessica was completely floored. "So do I," she said at last.

"He was going to come back, too, until you rushed in and spoiled everything!"

"Oh, but . . . I . . ." Jessica did not know what to say. Her hands began to tremble.

"You're just pig-headed, that's your problem!" Nat shouted. "You want to be a famous scientist, but you just don't *think*!"

Jessica gazed at him. It was true. Everything she had tried so far had gone wrong. Somehow, nothing had turned out the way she planned.

"I'm sorry, Nat," she said at last. "And I'm going to fix it. I promise."

"Oh, you are, are you?" Nat shouted. "Well, you've done a wonderful job so far! If it wasn't for you, they wouldn't be fighting now!"

And he turned around and fled into his bedroom, slamming the door behind him.

Jessica stayed on the stairs. She felt as still and cold as the pond slime in the fridge, and the worst of it was that she knew that Nat was right. Not only had she failed as a witch dispatcher, but rather than bringing her parents back together, she had driven them further apart.

With a hiccuppy gulp, Jessica began to cry. She clenched her hands and she squeezed her eyes tight and she held her breath, but she could not stop. The tears went on coursing down her cheeks, dripping off the end of her nose, and drizzling into her mouth.

With a howl, she leapt up and ran into her bedroom, where she hid her head under the pillow and sobbed and sobbed and sobbed.

After a while, she grew calmer. She wiped her face on her pillow and sat up and hugged her knees.

I've got to put things right, she thought. I must, I must, I must.

She began to think about everything that had happened, and she thought and thought until her brain hurt. But nothing came to her. At last she

crawled to the side of the bed, fished out her notebook from among the fluff underneath, and wrote:

*Nat is right, I am a failure. Plan A and Plan B went horribly wrong. They went worse than wrong. If it wasn't for Plan A, Mom would never have seen Miss Barnaby. And then Miss Barnaby wouldn't have been her first client. And then Miss Barnaby wouldn't have told all her friends. And then Mom wouldn't have had her second or her third client. But thanks to Plan A she did. Thanks to Plan A, it looks like Mom will be a very successful witch.*

*But Plan B was worse. If it wasn't for Plan B, Dad would have got Mr. Flotsam's contract. He would be about to become a successful garden designer. And he might have moved back in again. I can't believe it! Dad is miserable. And Nat is miserable. And I'm miserable. I think even Mom is miserable. And it's all my fault.*

A big teardrop plopped down on her writing, smudging it. Jessica rubbed it with her thumb and the smudge got worse. She picked up her pen again.

*I will make things right again, if it's the last thing I do!*

A little later there was a tap at the door. Nat came in. He was carrying a packet of snack cakes.

"Chocolate minirolls," he said gruffly. "From the top shelf, where Mom hides them. One good thing about Mom and Dad fighting, she didn't see me take them."

For a while, Jessica did not think she could eat a chocolate miniroll. But after she had watched Nat eat two, smearing Jessica's comforter with chocolate as he did so, she thought maybe she could. By the time she had eaten one, she felt more cheerful. By the time she had eaten two, she could feel her old determination welling up again.

"Nat," she said, "I know my plans didn't work out the way I thought. But it will be all right."

Nat looked at her. "How?"

"I'm not sure yet. But," she added in her most determined voice, "I'll figure it out. I promise you."

# Chapter Nine

The very next day Mr. Flotsam's article appeared. He must have rushed off and written it at once. He must still have been in a terrible mood when he wrote it, for it was extremely rude about Mrs. Haggerthwaite. It even called her a disgrace to the town.

"Bellstone is a thriving, modern metropolis," the paper thundered. "And this kind of old-fashioned hocus-pocus is a blot on our fair name. Witches are for wackos!"

Mrs. Haggerthwaite absolutely hated the article, and was very cross about it. In fact, when Jessica and Nat got back from school, they found her in such a bad mood that they decided to go straight over to Aunt Kate's.

Their aunt greeted them warmly, accompanied by a delicious aroma of apples, raisins, and cinnamon.

"Your dad's out in the greenhouse," she said, "moping over his tomatoes. I tell him he should stop worrying about them and start worrying about his family. And your mom is just as bad. I saw that article today. Such a lot of nonsense!" Aunt Kate tutted.

"That's what we think, too," said Jessica.

"Well, my loves, you tell them so. But first here's some apple cake for you. Hot from the oven. And don't worry," she added. "It will all work out in the end."

They found Mr. Haggerthwaite staking his plants. He did his best to produce a cheery grin when he saw them, but it was definitely drooping around the corners. Jessica looked at his tired face and past it to the sunlight breaking through the trees, and she wondered why, on such a beautiful afternoon, the Haggerthwaite family could not be happy together. Then she turned her attention to more practical matters.

"I'm sorry about that contract, Dad."

"Don't worry, love," Mr. Haggerthwaite said. "It wasn't your fault."

"Actually, it was." Jessica told him about Plan B. Mr. Haggerthwaite rumpled her hair.

"Still, you meant well."

Nat snorted. Jessica stared at her feet. "Dad," she asked, "won't you come home?"

A new expression crossed Mr. Haggerthwaite's face. To Nat, watching, it seemed mostly misery. But there was definitely some stubbornness there, too.

"Things aren't that simple," he said.

"Why aren't they?"

"Things have gone too far. Anyway, we shouldn't talk about this. It's nothing to do with you children. It's between your mother and me."

At this, Jessica grew very angry. "Of course it's to do with us! You're not even living at home! How do you think Nat and I feel about that?"

"We feel terrible," said Nat.

Mr. Haggerthwaite looked at them and his face seemed to crumple. "I suppose you're right. It's just . . . I can't come home."

"Is it because you can't forgive Mom about the contract?" asked Jessica.

"No—no, it's not that . . ."

"Is it because you don't like her being a witch?"

"No, I've gotten used to that . . ."

"Well, what is it then?"

Mr. Haggerthwaite sighed. "I don't know if you children would understand. It's just, well, I don't feel she has any respect for me anymore. I don't know how to explain . . ." His eyes fell on the plants in front of him. "I mean, take these tomatoes. I've been growing them all my life. But she doesn't even think I can do that. A couple of weeks ago she says she wants me to try some old magic she's found for cultivating fruits and vegetables. You mix up a potion and say some stupid spell or other, and then you pour the stuff on the roots, instead of the fertilizer and compost I always use. And then—hey, presto—a wonderful crop of tomatoes! As if the ones I've been growing all these years weren't good enough for her! As if she doesn't trust me in my craft."

He shook his head. "I told her what I thought. I said, 'Mel, I'm a gardener by trade, and I've been raising vegetables for years and years. And normal plant food and a nice, sunny spot in the greenhouse are plenty good enough for raising fine tomatoes'. I told her she should content herself with be-witching other things and leave garden produce to me." He sighed. "But she wouldn't listen. On and on about it she went."

Jessica stared at the tomato plants in front of her. They were green and tall, and the tomatoes that nestled in the leaves were round and almost ripe. They seemed a very silly thing to get upset about. Certainly she found it hard to believe that her father cared more about tomatoes than he did about her mother becoming a professional witch, or about Mr. Flotsam's contract. But she tried hard to see his point of view. Tomatoes were important to him. Come to think of it, Jessica was supposed to be doing a science project about plants herself. Maybe she should try and take more of an interest.

It was difficult, though, when she really wanted

to shout at him that they were just a bunch of stupid tomatoes.

"Are these our tomatoes from home?"

Mr. Haggerthwaite nodded. "Mostly. I tried to find room for as many as I could over here. I knew there was no point leaving them to your mother." He shrugged. "The rest have probably dried up and died by now."

Jessica frowned. For a moment, she thought she had a glimmer of an idea. Then it was gone. She shook her head. Anyway, she had one last question to ask. An important one. Far more important than stupid tomatoes.

"Dad. You do *want* to come home, don't you?"

"Of course I do!" cried Mr. Haggerthwaite, astonished that she should even ask. Then he swept them both up in a hug. Which was all very nice, thought Jessica, nestling close against his chest, but it didn't help much with finding a way to make it happen.

When Jessica and Nat arrived home, it was to the astonishing sight of hundreds of people crowding around their front door and spilling out into the path and the street beyond.

"It's that article!" Jessica gasped. "They must have come to exorcise her or throw her into a duck

pond!" And she ran as fast as she could toward the house, with Nat panting along behind her.

As they got closer they could see Mrs. Haggerthwaite. She was surrounded by people. But it soon became clear that she was being neither exorcised nor chased into a duck pond. Far from it.

"I've already said I can't see you all today. I don't have time. Now I'm going to pass around this piece of paper, and you must all write down your names and telephone numbers, and then I'll call you up and arrange appointments separately."

The crowd began to grumble. One woman said, "That's all very well, but these warts of mine can't wait."

"And I need that good luck charm for my exams tomorrow," said a student. "I came straight over, the second I read the *Gazette*."

Nevertheless, everyone got into line and began writing down their details. A lot of them were saying things to Mrs. Haggerthwaite like "I can't do Thursdays, you know" and "Do you have anything for ingrown toenails?" and "It's my new van—I'm sure it's cursed. I've had two scrapes and a flat tire since Friday. Do you think you could have a look?"

"I don't believe it!" said Jessica.

She looked at Nat, who began, "This is all—"

"—my fault! I know!" Jessica put her hands over her ears and ran into the house.

She went straight upstairs to start thinking of a new plan. But after she had stared at her notebook for fifteen minutes without having a single idea, she changed her mind. Instead, she decided to have a look in the Haggerthwaites' own greenhouse. Perhaps she could find something in there to use for her science project. After all, it was time she started to work on it. There had been so many things happening recently that she had almost forgotten.

The first thing that she saw, sitting on a shelf, were six fine, healthy tomato plants.

Jessica stared at them. She could not at all understand what they were doing there.

She was still staring when her mother came in. Mrs. Haggerthwaite was taken aback to see Jessica. So taken aback that she almost dropped the large, green watering can that she was holding.

"Well, I am glad all those people have gone," she said when she had regained her composure. "Not that I wasn't happy to see them. But it was a bit much, so many all at once—"

"Mom," Jessica interrupted. "What are you doing?"

Mrs. Haggerthwaite looked guilty. "Me? I'm not doing anything."

"What are you doing with that watering can?"

"I'm . . . er . . . watering these plants."

"But Mom, you're not interested in gardening.
You know you're not."

"I can take an interest, can't I?" said Mrs. Haggerthwaite defensively. Jessica regarded her suspiciously. She wondered whether her mother was
missing Mr. Haggerthwaite, and that was why she

was looking after his plants. But it did not seem likely. Mrs. Haggerthwaite, like her daughter, had a practical nature. Even if she was pining for her husband, she was unlikely to spend her time mooning around the greenhouse as a result. No. Something funny was going on.

And then Jessica's suspicions hardened into an idea. Her mother turned away for a minute and Jessica lifted the lid off the watering can. Inside was not water but a dark liquid. Jessica dipped one finger into it and sniffed. It had a strange, earthy aroma.

Typical, thought Jessica furiously. Absolutely typical! I knew it! She always has to be right. Well, this time she's not going to be. I'm going to make sure of that!

She removed her hand quickly as her mother turned back with some garden shears to snip a couple of wilted leaves from the healthy plants.

Feeling very cross, Jessica said, "This gardening is all very well, but it doesn't make up for that contract. The contract that you lost."

To her amazement, Mrs. Haggerthwaite did not snap at her, nor did she deny that it was her fault. Instead she replied quietly, "I know."

"Oh." Jessica was considerably taken aback. "Well. What are you going to do about it?"

"I don't know what I can do. Except somehow make Mr. Flotsam change his mind."

"How are you going to do that?" Still skeptical, Jessica waited scornfully to hear that her mother was planning to slip him a magic potion or cast a spell on him—which would do no good at all.

"I'm not sure. But, well, I've been meaning for a while to give a party."

"A party!"

"That's right. You know I didn't have my usual party last Halloween. We were too short of money. But my business is doing so well, I thought we could make up for it now." She looked at Jessica and, seeing she was about to argue, hurried on. "It would be a party to celebrate the business. I could invite my clients—a sort of thank-you, really. And my fellow witches, of course. I thought Mr. Flotsam could be the guest of honor. After all," she added wryly, "judging by this afternoon, I'll owe my success more to him than to anyone."

"And that's going to make him change his mind?"

"Of course it will!"

Mrs. Haggerthwaite sounded her usual confident self. Jessica wanted to be convinced, but she was not. She thought that if Mr. Flotsam was even half as important as Robbie made out, then he probably went to parties all the time. Probably much grander affairs than a party at the Haggerthwaites'. He was unlikely to be overwhelmed with gratitude at being Mrs. Haggerthwaite's guest of honor. Still, she supposed it was nice of her mother to try and put things right.

As for the tomatoes, though, she couldn't let her mother get away with it.

Slowly, it came to her as she gazed at the tomatoes, with their round, pink fruit. She looked at them until her eyes lost focus and everything in the greenhouse appeared pink. And she realized that she had just had the most marvelous, wonderful, magnificent, splendiferous idea.

It would solve everything. Well, almost everything. Everything that mattered, anyway. It would win the contract back for her father. It would sort out this witchcraft business, once and for all. And—this was the most important thing—it would bring her parents back together.

There was only one problem—and it was a big one, that was true. It meant that Jessica could not win the science competition. For a moment she wondered whether she could bear this. But then she gritted her teeth. It was a sacrifice, but it was worth it. And after all, she comforted herself, there would be lots more prizes in the future. The Nobel Prize, to name but one.

Jessica gave the most enormous grin. Then, without a word to her mother, she went racing back to the house. She was going to write down Plan C in her notebook.

# Chapter Ten

The following week Mrs. Haggerthwaite had hardly a moment to spare. Every day was booked solid with clients demanding love potions, good-luck talismans, cures for baldness, incantations of one type or another, protective amulets, reviving draughts, charms against vampires or acne, invigorating tonics, and health-giving elixirs. "I don't want to boast," Mrs. Haggerthwaite said beaming, "but my astounding success astounds even me!"

Even Jessica had to admit that this success had a good side. For one thing, it meant that some of those nasty bills could be paid, and the Haggerthwaites could stop worrying that their telephone or electricity was about to be cut off. For another, it meant that Mrs. Haggerthwaite did not notice what Jessica was up to.

For example, Jessica was spending a lot of time at Aunt Kate's. This was not remarkable in itself. Nat and Jessica often ran over to see their father and aunt. But it was certainly odd that Jessica should take a tape measure and a ball of string with her, and come home covered in soil.

Then there was Robbie Flotsam. He was forever coming over after school. Jessica said that they were working on their science projects together, and Mrs. Haggerthwaite thought nothing of it. But she should have remembered that Jessica had often told her that Robbie Flotsam was the nastiest boy she knew.

Then there were the footsteps on the stairs in the middle of the night. Not to mention the signs, afterward, that someone had been looking at Mrs. Haggerthwaite's spell book. Mrs. Haggerthwaite should certainly have noticed this. (She would have been absolutely furious, for nobody was allowed to look at her spell book except her.) But she was so tired from seeing all her new customers that she slept as heavily as if she had taken her own Guaranteed Effective Sleeping Potion.

Besides, she was under the fond impression that her spell book was untouchable. It was, after all, kept in a magic box, sealed with her strongest and most powerful enchantments. (It was only later that it emerged that these enchantments were neither strong enough nor powerful enough to stand up to Jessica and the bread knife.)

Still, if Mrs. Haggerthwaite did not notice something was afoot, somebody else did. Nat did not have the distractions of a successful witchcraft business. Even if he slept through the footsteps on the stairs, he certainly noticed the tape measure, the string, and the soil. And the presence of Robbie Flotsam (who had, after all, tried to jam Nat's head between the school railings on at least three separate occasions).

It did not take Nat long to realize that Jessica was up to something. And once he had realized this, he lost no time in confronting her.

That evening, as Jessica was working in her room, Nat flung open the door. He got straight to the point.

"What are you up to?"

Jessica, head bent over her calculator, jumped.

"I wish you would knock, not just burst in," she said crossly.

"If I knock, then I won't be able to catch you, will I?" Nat pointed out. "What are those? And what's all that?" He gestured toward the graph paper, the colored pencils, and the calculator.

"Oh, you wouldn't understand," said Jessica. Then she sighed. "I have a new plan. But—"

"—it's all gone horribly wrong," Nat finished for her. "Tell me about it."

So Jessica did. Nat did not understand all of Jessica's explanation, especially the bits that involved sheets of graph paper with squiggly lines all over them. But he understood the basics of what she was doing. And, much to his own amazement, he actually thought Plan C was a good idea.

"So what's bothering you?" he asked when she had finished. "I mean, it sounds all right to me. Better than your other plans, anyway."

"But look at the results! I need to show Mom she's wrong . . ."

"Why?"

"It's obvious—" Then Jessica stopped short. Her eyes took on a thoughtful expression. "Hmm. Perhaps you're right. There are possibilities. I'll have to think about this."

She went back to her graphs. Nat grinned and left her to it.

Three days later Jessica was hurrying through the school gate when she heard a shout. "Jessica! Wait for me!"

It was Robbie Flotsam.

Jessica was not terribly pleased to see him. She did not want him to think that they were still going to be friends now that the projects were finished. Already some people at school had noticed them going home together, and several people had tried to be funny about it. And it was not as if she needed his company. She had plenty of her own friends now at school.

Of course at first everybody (even Clare) had been terribly snooty about Jessica having a mother who thought she was a witch. There were giggles and whispers and a lot of cruel comments and stupid jokes. Nat had suffered, too. Jessica had stuck up for her mother (after all, your mother is your mother, even if most of the time you wish she wasn't). But she had had a bad time.

Then things had started to change. First one girl and then another had approached Jessica to say how much their own mother had benefited from Mrs. Haggerthwaite's Energy and Vitality Enhancing Elixir, or how pleased their granny or auntie had been with a lucky charm or an incantation. Soon some of the girls were asking if Jessica could tell fortunes or make good-luck charms, too. Although Jessica was not about to forget the way some of them had behaved toward her, it was nice to have people to talk to once again. Even the boys had been quite polite. Simon Johnson had actually offered Jessica five dollars to get her mother to turn Robbie Flotsam into a frog. (Regretfully, Jessica had declined this.) Although,

come to think of it, Robbie, too, was less unpopular than he had been. Perhaps that was because he was spending more time on his science project, and less time jamming other kids' heads between railings.

"What do you want?" she asked ungraciously. "After all," she added, "we've handed in the projects now."

Robbie looked dismayed. He opened his mouth but nothing came out, and Jessica could not help feeling sorry for him. But she could see Clare smirking at her from the other side of the gate, so she hardened her heart and said nothing.

"It's just . . . about the science projects . . ."

"Got a new boyfriend, Jessica?" It was Clare. She snickered as she said it, and for a moment Jessica felt absolutely mortified. She did not want any boyfriend, and most particularly she did not want Robbie Flotsam.

"Come on, Jessica." It was Pippa, arm in arm with Clare. "You don't want to bother with the likes of *him*." She giggled. "Come and talk to us."

Jessica did not even notice Robbie's face, which had filled with misery as he waited for her to walk away. She was overcome by a new feeling. Suddenly she was no longer mortified. She was plain mad.

"You weren't even speaking to me last week!" she shouted. "You two-faced ninnies!" She grabbed Robbie's arm. "Come on! We've no time for the likes of them. You come home with me."

She marched him rapidly out of the gates, ignoring the tide of giggles. Her anger lasted until they were around the corner. Then she let go of his arm and hastily stepped away.

"Stupid twits!" she said crossly. "They made me forget Nat. We'll have to wait and go back. What was it you wanted to say?"

"What? Oh, that . . ." Robbie was having trouble finding his tongue. "It's just . . . I've been thinking . . . it's not fair for you not to win the science competition. I mean, you did all the work. And you're best at science, not me."

Jessica was considerably surprised. She had never suspected Robbie Flotsam of having a conscience before. "Look, don't worry about it. We had a deal, remember? Anyway, I need your dad to be in a really good mood. It's part of my plan."

"I don't see why the science competition's going to put my dad in a good mood."

"It will when you win! It'll make your dad think you're really something. He'll be pleased to no end." She paused. "And then he'll give my dad that contract."

"My dad wouldn't think anything of me even if my project won the Nobel Prize," said Robbie gloomily. He stared at his feet and once again Jessica felt sorry for him. It occurred to her that however stupid and idiotic and plain selfish her parents might sometimes be, they never left her in any doubt that they thought something of her and Nat. In fact, more than something.

"He will," she said firmly. "My whole plan depends on it. Remember he's going to be guest of honor at Mom's party as well. If he's guest of honor *and* you've won the science competition, then surely even he's got to be a bit pleased?"

"Perhaps." But Robbie did not sound very sure. He hesitated, then blurted out, "What is your plan, anyway? Go on, Jessica. Tell me."

Now it was Jessica's turn to hesitate. So far she had told only one person about Plan C, and that was Nat. She wondered whether she could really trust Robbie Flotsam.

As if he read her thoughts, Robbie said, "I won't tell anyone. I promise."

"All right then," said Jessica at last. "But it's a bit difficult to explain. You'd better come home and see the tomatoes."

"The tomatoes?"

Jessica grinned. "Yes," she said. "They're more interesting than you'd think."

Nat acted quite resigned when he found out that they were walking back with Robbie Flotsam. Robbie had not picked on him for ages. But he was relieved when Jessica and Robbie rushed straight out to the greenhouse. Nat went to watch TV with Liverwort, and he did not see them again until an hour later, when he found them sitting on the steps that led down into the garden.

Robbie was saying, "Yeah, I see. Not bad! Not bad at all!"

Jessica looked smug and Nat sighed. He didn't think she needed any encouragement.

"I suppose it is quite clever," she said.

"It's magic!" Robbie grinned. "Sorry. But you're right, though. That project won't win the competition. Definitely not."

"It won't win," Jessica agreed. "But it might just succeed!"

Nat sat down beside them. He was relieved when they gave up talking about how brilliant Jessica was, and turned to more ordinary things, like Liverwort, who was hunting for insects on the paving stones below. At the other end of the garden Mrs. Haggerthwaite was piling old branches onto the bonfire she was building next to the compost heap. It was going to be for the party. The guests would be able to roast potatoes and apples and marshmallows on it. She had already hung magic lanterns from the shrubs and apple tree, and although they were not lit, they looked nice as they bobbed lightly in the breeze.

After a while Mrs. Haggerthwaite shouted that they were a load of lazybones, and why didn't

they help her build the bonfire? So, after some grumbling, they did. It was hard work, but fun. Robbie soon gave up clouting other people over the head with branches when he realized that there were three of them, and they would clout him hard back.

At last it was time for Robbie to go home and for Mrs. Haggerthwaite to start dinner. But none of them wanted to go indoors. Instead Mrs. Haggerthwaite fetched a tin of Aunt Kate's cookies. They were supposed to be for the party, but Mrs.

Haggerthwaite said a few less would make no difference either way. So they all sat on the steps and
munched, while Liverwort hopped around their
feet, eating the crumbs. There were squirrels chas-
ing each other along the wall and wood pigeons
cooing in the apple tree. The sun dropped lower
and lower in the sky.

It was an almost perfect evening.

But Nat knew that something was missing. And
he felt sure that Jessica—and even their mother—
knew it, too.

# Chapter Eleven

The day of the party arrived at last and, to Mrs. Haggerthwaite's delight, turned into a warm, clear evening. She had chosen the date for its full moon. There is nothing a witch likes better than a full moon.

The party was supposed to start at eight, and by ten past the Haggerthwaites' house was already heaving with guests. Some of them were clients, and these were fairly ordinary people on the whole. But most of the rest were witches, and they were not ordinary at all.

Jessica had forgotten how weird the witches were. She had not seen them for a long time. She had not even seen them last Halloween, as Mrs. Haggerthwaite had not held her usual party. Even

Mrs. Haggerthwaite had not seen much of them, as first she had not had the money, and then she had not had the time, for going to her usual magical conferences and conventions. But all the witches had heard about her turning professional, and had flocked to the party to see how it was working out.

They were not all called witches: Some of them were wise women, and there were seers, clairvoyants, fortune-tellers, psychics, healers, and simply "Those Possessed of Mysterious Powers." But whatever they were called, they still went in for the "same load of hogwash" as Aunt Kate called it. They all wore strange clothes, mostly black, and

horrible jewelry—things like necklaces made of goats' teeth. They had piercing stares, and they talked about the Cosmic Forces, and sometimes the Dark Powers, in ways that made Jessica feel uneasy.

Several of them had brought their pets. These were familiars, or magical helpers, and so naturally they could not be left at home. There were cats, of course, but also dogs, lizards, and even a guinea pig. Liverwort got rather nervous, especially of the lizards with their flickering tongues. Nat noticed this and tucked him into his pocket, where he could just peek out now and then to see what was going on.

"Thank goodness you're here," Jessica said, opening the door to find Aunt Kate on the doorstep. "Where's Dad?"

"He's struggling with that crate you insisted we bring," said her aunt. "He's probably put his back out."

Jessica rushed down the path and found her father clutching the crate in both arms while trying to fend off a huge dog. It was unclear whether the dog was friendly or hostile, but there was no doubt at all that he very much wanted to throw himself at Mr. Haggerthwaite's chest.

"What a brute!" said Mr. Haggerthwaite, as Jessica hurled some cookie and the dog went bounding after it. "Does it bite?"

"It's the High Witch of Salem's Doberman," Jessica told him. "He's supposed to be perfectly harmless."

"Harmless!" muttered Mr. Haggerthwaite. "Quick! Let's get inside before he comes back." And he followed Jessica into the house, between groups of excited witches.

"I'd forgotten how awful your mother's parties were," said Mr. Haggerthwaite as they reached Jessica's room. Out of the corner of his eye he saw a black shape on the landing. "It's that dog again!"

The dog gave a delighted bark and made for Mr.

Haggerthwaite, who dumped the crate on the floor and went bounding down the stairs, the dog hot at his heels.

"Come back!" Jessica yelled after him. Then, as he disappeared around the corner, she cried, "Meet me here in ten minutes!" She was not sure he heard. She gave a most witchlike curse and ran for the stairs. She could not believe that everything was going wrong already.

Still, the first thing was to find her mother. This took longer than Jessica would have liked, and when she did find her, gossiping away with a gaggle of witches, it was not at all easy to persuade Mrs. Haggerthwaite to come upstairs.

"Not now, Jessica!" she snapped. "Can't you see I'm busy?"

At long last, and with a great deal of grumbling, she agreed to come upstairs. Anxiously, Jessica marched her up to her room. But when she flung open the door, her father was not there.

"I knew he wasn't listening!" Jessica turned to her mother. "Wait here! I'll be back in a minute."

"I will do nothing of the kind!" Mrs. Haggerthwaite shouted after her. Jessica did not even stop to argue but plummeted down the stairs again to search for her father.

Everywhere there were witches, cackling, chat-

tering, and gobbling cake. Everywhere there were witches' familiars, barking, yowling, spitting, howling, squeaking, squawking, and gobbling cake. At last she saw a familiar face, but it was only Aunt Kate, who was arguing with the High Witch of Salem. The words "a load of old hogwash" came floating over the barks and yowls, but Jessica had heard it all before.

She spotted Nat holding Liverwort to his chest, standing in a circle of cats. Jessica was about to chase them off, but then someone grasped her arm.

"Hello, Jessica. I was hoping for a word."

Miss Barnaby was beaming at her.

"Oh, hello, Miss Barnaby. I'm afraid I'm a little busy at the moment. I don't suppose you've seen my dad anywhere, have you?"

"No," said Miss Barnaby, "but I saw your mother just a second ago. She was heading for the kitchen."

Jessica uttered her witchlike curse again, and then caught sight of Miss Barnaby's expression. There was an uncomfortable moment. Then Miss Barnaby said, "Jessica, I need to talk to you about the science competition."

"Oh!" Jessica forgot about her parents and Nat. She crossed her fingers and asked, "Have you decided on the winner? I thought you were going to announce the results last week." For she had counted on Mr. Flotsam having heard the good news by now.

"*You* are the winner, Jessica."

Miss Barnaby beamed. For a moment there was silence. Then Jessica let out a howl.

"But I can't be!"

"Of course you can! Don't be so modest, Jessica." Miss Barnaby smiled but she looked a bit puzzled. Jessica had never been known for her modesty. "It was an excellent project and deserved to win. I must admit, it was a very difficult decision —more difficult than I expected. That's why it's taken me so long. Two of the projects were really very good. But at the end of the day, yours was the best. So I thought I would tell you now, instead of waiting until Monday."

Miss Barnaby continued beaming in a kindly way, as if she was sure that she was making Jessica very, very happy indeed. Jessica gazed back with an expression of absolute horror.

"But I can't have won! I mean, my project was all about magic!"

"But very scientifically conducted. After all, that is the mark of a true scientist, Jessica. To keep an open mind to unusual ideas and then think of ways to test them impartially and rigorously." Jessica just scowled and Miss Barnaby lost confidence a little. "Aren't you . . . aren't you pleased?"

"Pleased? I think you may have ruined my life!"

Miss Barnaby gasped.

Jessica turned and disappeared into the crowd.

She was seething inside. That part of her plan— her beautiful plan—was ruined. Now she had better find her parents as quickly as possible, before anything else could go wrong.

And this time Jessica was in luck. For there, heading out of the back door into the garden, was her mother. And there, heading toward the back door out of the garden, was her father.

It was now or never.

# Chapter Twelve

This time Jessica allowed no time for argument. With a flying leap she went through the back door, grabbing her mother by her long, flowing, witchlike scarf as she passed. As she landed, she grabbed her father by his ordinary, gardenerlike denim collar.

"Right," she announced. "You two are coming with me."

Mr. and Mrs. Haggerthwaite looked at Jessica, then looked at each other. Then, like two lambs, they meekly followed their daughter into the house and upstairs into her bedroom. They could both see that there was absolutely no point in fighting.

"This had better be good," said Mrs. Haggerthwaite, recovering her composure somewhat.

Jessica ignored her.

"Sit down," she commanded.

She waited until her parents were sitting attentively on her bed. Then she went over to the crate her father had brought and undid the string. She lifted the lid and carefully, very carefully, one by one, lifted out the contents. Then she reached behind her desk and lifted out six more of the same type of object.

"Tomatoes!" Mrs. Haggerthwaite looked very puzzled.

"Tomato plants," Mr. Haggerthwaite corrected her. "And very fine ones, too. I'm sure that's because Jessica keeps them in a sunny part of the greenhouse and uses the best fertilizer . . ."

"*Be quiet!*" Jessica yelled. Her parents were so startled that they did. Jessica stood facing them in front of her tomato plants.

"Now listen to me. This is my science project. And you're going to pay attention while I explain it to you.

"As you can see, there are twelve plants. Six are from Aunt Kate's greenhouse, and six are from our greenhouse here at home. They all came from seeds that Dad originally grew in our greenhouse. But six of them Dad took to Aunt Kate's and has been raising *his* way. And six are the ones that got left behind and Mom has been raising them *her* way."

With that, Mr. Haggerthwaite gave Mrs. Haggerthwaite a very accusing look. She had the grace to blush a little.

"Well, why not?" she began. "After all, you weren't needing them . . . " Jessica silenced her with a glare.

"These tomatoes," Jessica continued, "were raised from the same soil and from the same packet of seed—even the amount of sunlight was the same. I checked all those things. There was only one difference. Dad's six plants were treated with normal fertilizer. But Mom's six were treated with her magic potion."

Her parents sat gazing at her in silence, and Jessica took a deep breath and continued her explanation.

"Now, every scientific experiment needs to have a hypothesis. That's what you think is going to happen, or what you're trying to prove," she added, seeing her parents look blank. "My hypothesis"—and here she blushed a little—"was that the plants treated with the fertilizer would grow faster than the plants treated with Mom's potion."

"Typical!" Mrs. Haggerthwaite snorted.

"Well," said Jessica, almost apologetically, "you

know I want to be a scientist. Of course I thought fertilizer was best. I wanted to prove you wrong, once and for all. And I thought that this was the one thing that might make you see sense." She paused. "After all, I *am* a witch dispatcher."

"If you mean that ridiculous sign on your door . . ." began Mrs. Haggerthwaite dangerously. But Mr. Haggerthwaite hushed her.

"Go on, love," he said, turning to Jessica.

"So I measured them all very carefully—in fact I measured every tomato plant in both greenhouses—several times, and I wrote it down in my notebook, and I made my bar chart . . ."

Mr. and Mrs. Haggerthwaite were no longer listening. They were staring at the tomato plants.

"But they're all exactly the same!" Mrs. Haggerthwaite burst out.

"I know," said Jessica. "They're exactly the same height. Whether you used fertilizer or magic potion, it didn't make any difference. And on average they produced the same number of leaves and the same number of tomatoes, too. And," she added, just so there should be no remaining doubts, "Nat and I took turns being blindfolded, and then we tested a tomato from every plant, and they taste equally delicious, too."

There was a long silence.

Then both Mr. and Mrs. Haggerthwaite burst into speech. Was Jessica sure she had got it right? Had she really measured the plants the right way? Had she really counted every leaf? Had she really tasted the tomatoes?

"Of course I did!" Jessica declared crossly. "And Miss Barnaby said the whole thing was completely scientific. After all," she added, "I have won first prize in the science competition!"

And before her parents could say anything else, she went on, "And I did more than that, too. I found out *why* they're the same height."

"How on earth did you do that?" asked her father.

"Easy," said Jessica. "I got hold of Mom's spell book—"

"You did what?" Mrs. Haggerthwaite glared.

"—And then I looked up the ingredients in my *Junior Science Encyclopedia*. And what I discovered is that a lot of her potion is the same thing, really, when it comes to the actual *chemicals*, as Dad's fertilizer. Like the comfrey. There's lots of comfrey in Mom's potion, and comfrey's just full of potassium."

"Tomatoes love potassium," said Mr. Haggerthwaite.

"I know," said Jessica. "And then there's the soaked nettles. They have potassium, too, and so do the sow thistles. And the sorrel has calcium and phosphorus. And then there's the seaweed."

"Seaweed!"

"Yes. Seaweed has *everything*! It's wonderful! They even sell it at the garden center. Mind you," she added, "I'm not sure about the dead beetles. Or the pond slime. Or the sheep's eyes."

"I left those out, actually," Mrs. Haggerthwaite admitted.

"So it's not surprising that the plants grew to the same height," said Mr. Haggerthwaite.

"Not really. Mrs. Lippitt at the garden center says the potion is probably what they would call an organic fertilizer. It does the same thing as a commercial fertilizer, but it has all natural ingredients."

"And you've always been in favor of organics, Tom!" Mrs. Haggerthwaite pointed out smugly.

"Well, of course, if I'd known you were just talking about an organic fertilizer—"

"Not *just* an organic fertilizer," Mrs. Haggerthwaite corrected him. "An ancient, long-treasured magic potion, that, it just so happens, can also be explained in modern scientific terms. A victory for witchcraft, I would say! And how do these chemicals make the tomatoes grow, eh? Tell me that! There's the real magic!"

Jessica grinned. And, having watched the tomato plants herself, and seen their hard, green spheres turn into ripe, red fruit, she almost wondered if her mother was right. But she did not want to be distracted.

"Now you listen to me," she told her parents. "I don't care one bit about tomatoes! Not a whisker, not a smidgen. As Aunt Kate would say, I don't give a hoot!"

"But then why—" began Mr. Haggerthwaite, rather startled.

"I'll tell you why." And suddenly Jessica found her voice was shaking. "Because I care that you don't live here anymore! And I wanted to work out your stupid arguments, once and for all!"

She gestured toward the tomato plants.

"You can see the truth before you. You were both right and you were both wrong. And perhaps that's true of other things, too. Maybe that's something you should think about." She swallowed. "And now . . . well, I can't stop you living apart if you want to, or even"—she clenched her hands—"getting a divorce. But if you do get divorced, don't pretend it's over something as stupid as how to grow tomatoes."

All of a sudden, Jessica was sure she was going to burst into tears. Blinking furiously, she turned and fled from the room. Behind her she could hear her parents calling, "Jessica! Jessica! Come back!" but she paid no attention.

It's up to them now, she thought as she stumbled across the landing and down the stairs. It's up to them. I've done my very best, and now it's really up to them.

# Chapter Thirteen

Jessica found that she was feeling quite shaky as well as ravenously hungry. So she set off toward the kitchen, where she and Nat had hidden a secret supply of cookies, well out of the way of even the greediest witch.

But not, it seemed, of Mr. Flotsam. He was standing next to an empty cookie tin, chewing, with a very smug expression on his face.

"Whhah! Wewwicca!"

Jessica jumped. For a moment she thought it was some kind of spell. Perhaps he had chosen to go into the magical line himself, now that he knew there was money to be made from it. But then he swallowed his cookie and cried, "Ah, Jessica! Good to see you! Try some of these!"

"There are none left," said Jessica pointedly.

"Oh . . . so there aren't. Never mind. They were delicious, though." He nudged Robbie, who was standing next to him. Robbie glowered but Mr. Flotsam did not seem to notice. Jessica was about to leave but Mr. Flotsam stopped her by coming up and grabbing her shoulder, with a friendly yet vise-like grip.

"Dad's got something to say to you," Robbie said. He stopped glowering and grinned. But of course, Jessica remembered, he didn't yet know about the science competition.

"That's right." Mr. Flotsam licked the crumbs from around his mouth. "Well, young lady, it seems you've been spending a lot of time with Robbie here. Helping him with his science project and all. Why, your Miss Barnaby was telling me just now that Robbie is a new boy! He couldn't even switch a computer on, a couple of months ago. But now there's no stopping him!"

"Don't—" Robbie began, embarrassed.

"So it seems to me that you deserve some kind of reward. And I seem to remember there was something you were rather keen on. That contract your dad was after—the one to landscape the grounds of my hotels . . ."

He had let go of Jessica, but she stayed rooted to the floor.

"You mean . . . you mean you're going to give Dad the contract?"

"I certainly do!"

"But Mr. Flotsam," whispered Jessica, hardly able to believe what she was hearing, "Robbie didn't win the science prize. I'm afraid . . . I'm afraid *I* did."

"Oh, I know that."

"You do?"

"Yes, Miss Barnaby told us just now, didn't she Robbie? But I don't care about the stupid prize. Nor does Robbie. No, the fact is, you've been a friend to him! And if there's one thing we Flotsams know, it's how to stand by our friends." He leaned forward and whispered confidentially (but in such a penetrating whisper that Jessica was sure Robbie could hear every word), "The boy doesn't have many friends, you know. He's not a popular boy. I don't pretend to understand children, and since his mother left, well . . ." He shook his head, then continued, "Robbie's been a complete pain in the neck ever since we came here. It's knowing you that's made all the difference."

Behind Mr. Flotsam, Robbie was blushing furiously. Jessica could tell that at that second, more than anything else on earth, he wanted to murder his father. But at the same time she knew that what Mr. Flotsam said was true.

"Anyway," Mr. Flotsam added, rather spoiling the moment, "I was always going to give your dad that contract. He's the best for the job, and that's what counts in business. I just thought I'd pay back your mother by making him sweat a bit first."

Jessica was not even listening. She burst out, "Thank you! I'll never forget this, never!" She was about to run for the door when Robbie grabbed her arm.

"There's more. Go on, Dad, tell her the other part."

"What's that? Oh yes." Mr. Flotsam calmly wiped his mouth. "We thought this project of yours —something to do with tomatoes, Robbie said it was—anyway, we thought that might make an interesting story, too."

"Story?" repeated Jessica, completely blank.

"Yes, for the *Gazette*. Not a front-page story, of course. But something on the inside, for kids. You know, explaining the experiment you did, and what you found out, and how they might do something similar at home. Of course nobody ever reads those kinds of stories," added Mr. Flotsam, un-flatteringly, "because kids find them boring. But parents like to know they're there. Makes them think they're buying something educational."

Jessica did not care how many people read the story. She would read it and she would make sure that Mr. and Mrs. Haggerthwaite and Nat and Aunt Kate did, too. And anyone else she met for the next hundred years. After all, it would be her first ever scientific publication.

She was too stunned even to thank Mr. Flotsam. At last she gasped, "Mr. Flotsam . . . Robbie . . . I *have* to go and tell Mom and Dad. You do understand, don't you? I mean, I don't want to be rude, but I just have to tell them!"

"Hey, wait for me!" Unexpectedly, Nat popped out from beneath the kitchen table, grinning. He was clutching Liverwort in one hand and in the other, a large piece of cookie. Jessica was too excited even to comment on this. She was already out the door.

They raced up to her bedroom. But her parents were no longer there. Nor were they on the landing, in the hall, or the living room. Jessica even checked the coat closet and interrupted Miss Barnaby, sitting and holding hands with a man who had the most adoring expression on his face. But Jessica had no time for them.

They ran into the garden but all they found was a bunch of hungry witches, gobbling roast potatoes. Jessica scoured the garden back and forth—it did not take long, for it was not a big garden. But she could not find her parents anywhere. They were not sitting on the back doorstep. They were not on the patio. They were not in the greenhouse. They were not standing around the bonfire. Nor were they behind the rhododendron (the only shrub the garden possessed) or under the apple tree (the only tree). They weren't anywhere.

At last Jessica and her brother sat down on the grass under the apple tree.

"Did you show them the tomatoes?" Nat asked. Jessica nodded.

"Oh, well then, they're probably having a fight about how to grow begonias now," said Nat gloomily.

It seemed all too likely. For a few moments they sat in silence and watched some of the younger witches, who seemed to have drunk rather too much of Mrs. Haggerthwaite's nettle ale, dancing around the bonfire.

"What else has been going on?" asked Jessica at last.

Nat snorted. "Not a lot. Aunt Kate is arm-wrestling with the High Witch of Salem."

Despite her worries, Jessica grinned. "Who's winning?"

"Aunt Kate won. But now the High Witch says it's best of three."

They caught each other's eyes and began to laugh. They rolled around in the grass and threw leaves at each other. Jessica was getting a stomachache, she was laughing so hard. And suddenly she realized that someone else was laughing, too. It wasn't Nat, who was giggling into a tree root. In fact it sounded like more than one person. Jessica fell back against the tree's trunk, still laughing, and then she stopped short.

For it was then that she saw the foot hanging out of the sky.

# Chapter Fourteen

It was a familiar foot. And any wild ideas Jessica might have had about witches and broomsticks were immediately ended. For the foot was attached to a leg, and it was dangling from the branches of the apple tree.

Jessica peered up into the leaves. And finally, as the flames of the bonfire roared up behind her, she made out that there was not just one figure sitting there but two. They were familiar figures. And they were grinning at her.

"Mom!" she yelled. "Dad!" And then, in a great rush and a jumble, she began to tell them all about Mr. Flotsam and the landscaping contract and the newspaper article.

"It's great, isn't it?" Jessica finished. Then she

remembered that she had been hunting for them for ages and getting worried, too. "And what do you think you're doing up there?" she added sternly. "You can't run away from your own party, you know! I've been looking for you everywhere."

Her parents did not seem too upset by this. They just looked at each other and chuckled.

Nat nudged Jessica. "Look! They're holding hands!"

Mrs. Haggerthwaite blushed and Mr. Haggerthwaite winked at them. Not that they could really make out the wink in the dim light, but they just knew that he would have.

"It was a bit crowded inside," said Mrs. Haggerthwaite loftily, as if this explained everything. But she did not let go of Mr. Haggerthwaite's hand. And they were sitting very close together.

Jessica had a question, though she knew it might spoil everything. But she wanted to ask so badly.

Luckily, Nat asked for her.

"Dad," he whispered, "are you coming home?"

"Well," said Mr. Haggerthwaite, "we've been talking about it. Of course, first we had another look at the tomato plants, and I decided that mine had shinier, healthier leaves, and your mom decided that hers had rounder, redder tomatoes . . ."

Jessica and Nat groaned.

"But—well, it also seems to us both that Jessica was right about one thing. There is more to life than tomatoes."

"So you are coming back!"

"I think that's for your mom to say," said Mr. Haggerthwaite.

There was a pause, during which Jessica and Nat gazed up into the leaves, desperately trying to make out Mrs. Haggerthwaite's expression. After a moment, Mr. Haggerthwaite said, "In case you didn't see, that was definitely a nod."

Then there was a lot of confusion. Nat tried to climb the tree and fell off, and Mr. Haggerthwaite hauled him up, and Mrs. Haggerthwaite jumped down and hugged Jessica and jumped up again, and Jessica climbed up, and there wasn't enough room, and Nat nearly fell off again, and then, somehow, Nat ended up half on Jessica's lap and Mrs. Haggerthwaite was sitting on Mr. Haggerthwaite's, and the branch was shaking and creaking like anything. Everyone was giggling and talking at once. In the middle of it all there was an indignant croak and Liverwort stuck his head out of Nat's pocket, looking, insofar as a toad's complexion allows, very pale. Obviously, as Mr. Haggerthwaite pointed out, he wasn't a tree toad. But Mrs. Haggerthwaite took

him and cooed over him a bit and he soon looked happy again.

Then Jessica told them about her various plans, and how everything had gone so horribly wrong before (with a bit of help from Nat and Robbie) turning out for the best after all.

"And Mr. Flotsam did give you the contract, Dad," she finished. "Even though I won and not Robbie. Because he said that you were the best."

"Of course that contract hardly matters now that I've got a witch tycoon for a wife," Mr. Haggerthwaite joked. But everybody could see that it did matter and that he was terribly, terribly pleased.

"And now," said Mrs. Haggerthwaite, "I have something to say."

There was a sudden silence while Jessica and Nat gazed at her, wondering what came next.

"I have come to realize," Mrs. Haggerthwaite told them, "that my—um—new career has made things very awkward for all of you. Of course I knew Jessica hated it right from the start. But with Nat being teased at school and you, Tom, nearly losing that contract—well, I know things have been difficult. I should at least have consulted you before I went into business."

"That's all right, love," Mr. Haggerthwaite began, but Mrs. Haggerthwaite stopped him.

"It's not all right. We're a family, after all. But I'm going to make up for it now. I'm asking you all what you think, and if you say the word, then I'll go back to being an ordinary amateur witch again."

There was a brief pause.

Then Mr. Haggerthwaite said, "Don't be silly, Mel! Your clients all love you. And anyone can see you love the job! Of course you should keep going!"

Nat said, "It's all right, Mom. Nobody teases me anymore. Even Robbie Flotsam's nice to me these days."

Everyone looked at Jessica.

Jessica closed her eyes. Surely this was the moment she had been waiting for? The final, crowning success of her career as a professional witch dispatcher! All she had to do was say the word, and her mother would give up witchcraft—at least in her professional capacity—forever. It would just be her crazy little hobby again and nobody would have to know about it. After all, now that her father had won the contract, they would not even need the money.

And yet, somehow she didn't say it.

Everybody *did* know, after all. Why, Mrs. Haggerthwaite was famous throughout Bellstone! And it was true that nobody really minded. In fact, a lot of people thought it was great. And as for the

rest—well, Jessica did not really care anymore what Clare, or a few people like her, thought. Anyway, when Jessica became famous and had her picture in the paper . . . But she already was a famous scientist! Her story *was* going to be in the paper! So who cared what anyone thought!

Her mother did enjoy being a witch. And Jessica herself had shown—scientifically, too—that there might be something in it after all.

All along she had thought that witch dispatching would bring her parents back together. It hadn't worked out quite like that. And yet her parents *were* back together. Jessica was no longer sure that anything else mattered.

"It's all right, Mom," she said, with sudden relief. "If you're crazy enough to want to be a witch, then that's fine with me."

"Thank you, Jessica," said Mrs. Haggerthwaite. And Mr. Haggerthwaite and Nat cheered.

There followed a lot more talking and giggling. The party was almost over, but the stars and moon were bright above them when at long last the Haggerthwaites jumped down from the tree. They went to roast marshmallows and talk and joke together until the very last ember had gone out, and the very last witch had been woken and had found her dog or cat or lizard and gone home.

In the middle of the night, Jessica woke up and suddenly remembered her Witch Dispatcher sign. She climbed out of bed and turned on her desk lamp. Grabbing a pen from her desk, she opened her bedroom door.

In the next room, Jessica knew, Nat was asleep with Liverwort on the pillow beside him. And across the hall, in the room with the big double bed, not only her mother but her father, too, was sleeping off the exhaustion caused by the best party the Haggerthwaites had ever had.

Jessica gave a contented sigh.

Then she took her pen and carefully altered her sign.

**JESSICA HAGGERTHWAITE
PROFESSIONAL WITCH DISPATCHER
(RETIRED)**

Then Jessica went back to bed.